TRAIL WOLVES

On the last day of the war, Davis was looking forward to some peace. However, Bradford had other ideas . . . They'd captured a Yankee wagon full of guns and Bradford knew that, in Mexico, rebels paid high prices for weapons. Davis just wanted to return to his ranch in the Big Bend country. But Bradford wanted to stop him — as did the Yankees, the Mexican rebels and government troops. Davis would have no choice but to take them all on as they came . . .

CLAYTON NASH

TRAIL WOLVES

Complete and Unabridged

LINFORD
Leicester

First published in Great Britain in 2006 by
Robert Hale Limited
London

First Linford Edition
published 2007
by arrangement with
Robert Hale Limited
London

British Library CIP Data

Nash, Clayton
    Trail wolves.—Large print ed.—
    Linford western library
    1. Western stories
    2. Large type books
    I. Title
    823.9'14 [F]

    ISBN 978–1–84617–740–8

Published by
F. A. Thorpe (Publishing)
Anstey, Leicestershire

Set by Words & Graphics Ltd.
Anstey, Leicestershire
Printed and bound in Great Britain by
T. J. International Ltd., Padstow, Cornwall

This book is printed on acid-free paper

1

Damn Yankees!

It was almost noon and Davis, on guard, was chasing the vanishing shade amongst the heat-shimmering boulders. He had just found a cool, dark patch and was settling down with his battered old Spencer carbine, lifted from a dead Yankee more than three years ago now, when he heard the call from below.

It was just a sound at first, a human voice drifting up from the floor of the canyon, echoing a little from the ramparts up here. Then, as he paused, holding his breath while he listened, he made out the words.

And his blood ran cold.

'You up there, Reb?'

Judas priest! What the hell was a Yankee doing in here, calling that way . . . ?

'Reb! We know you and your friends hole up somewhere over this way! I mean you no harm! Look!'

Davis was already looking — cautiously — and he saw the rider down below in a clearing in the rocks, his uniform blue and dusty and generally saddle-worn. He had a weathered campaign hat on his head and he knocked it slightly askew as he waved the pole with the white flag attached to the top.

'What's he doin'? Surrenderin'?'

Davis knew it was Chet Bradford by the voice, so didn't turn his head. His eyes narrowed as he nodded, watching that Yank closely. He heard the others coming out of cover now, Curly Keller whistling softly through his teeth. Matheson hawked and spat, cocked the side hammer on his well-used but mighty deadly Hawken muzzle-loading rifle.

'Can knock him right out from under that there hat,' he opined in his raspy voice. 'No trouble at all.'

'Hey! That's a white flag!' It had to be Boone who said that: he was still not out of his teens although he had been riding with the Trail Wolves for two years.

Matheson spat again. 'So? I'd like to see some red on it — *blood* red.'

'Dammit, Matt, it's a flag of truce!'

'Time you learned the facts of life, Boone!'

Bradford reached out and cupped a hand over the Hawken's big hammer. He shook his head at Matheson and that was all it took. The man lowered the gun. 'White flag — but that's still a damn Yankee down there, Chet!'

'Let's see what he wants.' Bradford, a big man, shouldered Davis aside easily, although Davis was just as big and hard-muscled. But he did it arrogantly, without thought — he was the leader so it was his right to take the best position to observe. *And don't forget it!* 'He alone, Link?'

'I never had a chance to look,' Davis told him, meeting the slow turning of

Bradford's head and the hard stare with a coolness in his own grey eyes.

'Well, look now.'

'You look. You've got the best spot.'

Bradford stared and then grinned. 'So I should . . . ' He writhed around a little, lifting his upper body warily. As the man below called again he lowered himself and shook his head. 'Din' see nobody else — '

'Light haze off to your right,' Davis said, pointing with the rust-patched barrel of his Spencer. 'Could be a small troop — or a wagon.'

'What'd that sunnabitch say?' Keller asked. 'Couldn't catch it with you two old women maggin' away.'

'He said,' began Boone, licking his lips, his buckteeth prominent and his eyes beginning to bulge. 'By Godfrey! He said: 'The war's over!' That's it! That's what he said!'

In his excitement, Boone jumped up and started waving his hat before anyone could stop him. 'Hey, Yank! Say that again!'

Matheson hit him across the back of the knees with the heavy barrel of the Hawken and Boone grunted as he sprawled. 'Idiot! He coulda shot you. *Should've*, actin' that way!'

The Yankee looked a little wary now as he found them, saw the rifle barrels covering him. He held his flagpole high and lifted his other hand above his head.

'It's true! Lee capitulated five or six days ago — signed his surrender at Appomattox! I have it here in a copy of *Harper's Weekly*.' Carefully, he pulled a folded and tattered magazine from inside his tunic and waved it. 'I'll read it to you.'

'Leave it on the rock! We're only ignorant Rebs but a couple of us can read!' called Bradford, his hands working sweatily on the action of his Henry rifle which had seen better days — and a lot of killing.

'My apologies, Reb.' The Yankee officer leaned from the saddle, placed the magazine on top of a nearby boulder, straightened in his saddle. 'I'm Major Lyall Reece of the Third Pennsylvania Regiment. We're a long way from home and it's been a long war. Your band has fought hard, given us more than one headache. But it's over now, gents. I should take you in, but, as I said, it's over. Make your ways to your homes as best you can. There'll be hard times ahead, I'm thinking, for all of us. But you fought well and can be proud of your records. Good luck!'

He waved, then turned to ride off. Bradford called: 'How'd you figure to take us in, Yank? With the help of that troop you're hidin' over there under the dust cloud?'

Major Reece hauled rein, stood in his stirrups, shading his eyes. Then he settled back into leather and said, easily: 'That's only a wagon escort. They were heading for Fort McKenzie when I brought them the news. You've nothing to fear from them or any other Union soldier. Hostilities have ended!'

'Not . . . quite!' said Bradford. He

nodded to Matheson who was already sighting down the flat top of the Hawken's octagonal barrel, horny thumb snapping back the side hammer.

'No, dammit!' snapped Davis, his face hard as he looked at Bradford, started to move in on Matheson.

Too late.

The Hawken boomed its cannon-like thunder and a thick cloud of white smoke swirled from the blackpowder charge, briefly hiding the rider below. When it cleared, Major Lyall Reece was sprawled on the ground, unmoving, a large splash of blood showing between the shoulders of his dilapidated tunic. The horse ran off.

The white flag was crumpled in the dust, but there were a few splashes of bright red showing amongst the grime.

★ ★ ★

'What I want to know is what they've got in that damn wagon,' Chet Bradford said tightly, lowering the battered field glasses. 'Must be somethin' important to have so many outriders.'

'Too many for us, anyway,' Keller said, scratching at his ear.

Bradford bent an eyebrow at the swarthy man as Keller ran a hand absently over his jowls; as long as any of them had known him, Curly Keller had shaved every second day without fail. His razor's blade was well-worn with use but he sharpened it again and again on any handy leather and kept his jowls mostly smooth. It was hard work, him being so dark of skin. With his jet-black hair and deep, glittering eyes, he looked more Mexican than Kentuckian.

'Wait a spell,' Bradford said, looking through the glasses again. 'Think they're splittin' up. Some kind of palaver goin' on — argument, looks like. The officer — hell it's a lieutenant! — seems to be tryin' to stop 'em.'

'Takin' Reece's word as gospel and headin' for home, I guess,' opined Matheson, fingering his reloaded Hawken.

Bradford nodded slowly, still using the glasses. 'Uh-huh. More'n half are ridin' out. Loot's reachin' for his gun but . . . Well, hell almighty! They shot him!'

They heard the dull crack of two pistol shots and even without the field glasses they saw the officer blown out of his saddle. Then the argument started up again and it was clear there were two separate trains of thought here: the larger group wanted to ride back the way they had come, north, towards their distant homes. The smaller group seemed to want to stay with the wagon.

'If they had a lieutenant in charge,' Keller said thoughtfully, 'must be *somethin'* important in that wagon.'

'Yeah — and we're gonna find out what it is.'

Davis snapped his head towards Bradford. 'Haven't you had enough fighting, Chet?'

'Never have enough,' Bradford replied cheerfully. 'No, we'll let the big group get under way, then pick up the wagon somewhere along the trail, well out of range so the shootin' don't bring back their pards.'

Davis was already unsettled by the cold-blooded killing of Reece and he *wanted* to believe it was true about the war ending. He was a long way from home in the Big Bend country and he was itching to get started in that direction.

They had been guerrillas for three years, harassing the Yankees wherever they could find them, earning themselves the title of 'The Trail Wolves', the name itself bringing many a Union soldier out in goosebumps. They had been picked for their marksmanship and hardness, their loyalty to the Confederacy, and they had caused havoc wherever they struck. But somewhere along the line, communications with headquarters had broken down and they were left to their own devices. Bradford, being a sergeant, assumed command and it wasn't long before they were operating as just an independent band of raiders, grabbing every chance not to only attack the Yankees and their sympathizers, but to line their own pockets as well. In short, they were no better than a bunch of outlaws, but they never did attack anyone connected with the Confederacy, although there had been temptations. But Davis's objections had been so strong that Bradford hesitated to call him out. Davis put it plainly enough:

'We're still Johnny Rebs. We've got a lousy rep as it is with the damn Yankees. We get that same rep with our own people and we've got nothing. No future. Just a rope or a bullet waiting.'

'We got them now,' argued Bradford, but everyone knew he was already wavering.

'*Yankee* rope or bullets,' Davis pointed out. They could see he wasn't going to back down, was prepared to precipitate a gunfight if necessary.

'Aaah, we're doin' all right, I guess,'

Bradford said and it was settled.

For now.

But the others noticed Davis didn't relax for a long time. And they knew Bradford wasn't going to forget this moment.

'You can do with a stake to take back to Texas, can't you?' Bradford said persuasively. 'That wagon must be loaded with goodies to've had a big escort like that. C'mon! One last strike for the good ol' boys! Singe the Yankees' britches one more time then to hell with 'em all. It's the homebound trail afterwards!'

That suited them all, even Davis reluctantly agreeing he could use some hard cash to take back to his ailing father on the old spread.

So it was settled and they lay low, watching the Yankees split up. They posted a man — Boone, young but also with young vision — on the ramparts to watch the direction the wagon and its escort of some eight remaining soldiers took while the others rested in the shade. By mid-afternoon Bradford reckoned the main group of soldiers were far enough off not to hear any gunfire; there was no dispute that there *would* be gunfire.

'That wagon ought to be headin' towards Musket Pass by now,' Bradford said. 'We'll go wait for 'em. Ought to hit 'em about sundown and they'll be ridin' straight into the west.'

Bradford was a killer, but he was a smart one and mighty good at tactics. It was something that came naturally to him and Davis figured the planned attack had been fully formed in the man's mind the moment he had decided to go after the wagon.

★   ★   ★

There were mules drawing the heavily laden army wagon, a string of six. Matheson shot one of the leads and that stopped the wagon and its escort dead in their tracks.

There was a man with corporal's stripes

down there, a grizzled, experienced-looking man, and before the thunderous echoes of the Hawken had died, he was shouting orders in a voice that had been roughened by many years of frontier booze and raw, harsh tobacco.

'Cover! Cover!' He shaded his eyes against the setting sun's glare, turning his head this way and that to get the best view possible. Amber light flashed from a lifting rifle barrel. 'Not that side, goddamnit! Hit the shade, you bunch of schoolboys! Keep the sun outta your eyes!'

'Schoolboys' was probably some sort of Yankee insult because none of the men looked younger than mid-twenties, and old army hands, too. They hit the grit and started raking the rim with gunfire even though they couldn't have spotted any real targets so quickly. But flying bullets made any man smart enough keep his head down if he was within ten yards of where they were landing. Two troopers reared up and fell.

The Wolves were on both rims of the pass and the guns hammered, Davis's old Spencer making its two-planks-hitting-together sound as the big .56 calibre bullets chewed up the rock. The mules were braying and honking, fighting and tangling themselves in the traces. The wagon hardly rocked and the springs were compressed almost straight, so whatever it was carrying must weigh plenty.

Davis lifted his carbine as lead sprayed grit into his face. He reared back, instinctively pulling the trigger, cursing that he had wasted a shot. All he had was about five more cartridges left in the old tin magazine he had slapped into the butt of the Spencer. The retaining clip was busted and he kept a special whittled wedge of bear-claw to jam under the end of the tube and hold it in place. Sometimes the jar of recoil caused it to come loose and there was a frantic scramble to find the tube and shove it back into the butt, hoping it hadn't been dented badly enough to stop the smooth passage of the cartridges to the breech.

But it happened this time, and as he scrabbled around to look for the wedge he stood on the tube, mashing in the thin tinplate, effectively making it useless.

He flung the carbine aside and palmed up his Remington Army .44 pistol which he had taken off a Yankee officer he had killed in a hand-to-hand fight back in the Blue Mountains of Kentucky a year ago. He used both hands to steady the weapon — the Remington was a fine, accurate gun but the butt was too small and seemed to have been designed for youths or women rather than rough-handed Johnny Rebs.

He beaded a man down there, trying to run along the bottom of a small crevice, fired and saw the man's hat jump, the hair lift violently before he crashed out of sight. The revolver still smoking, Davis swung it along the line, came to rest on the grizzled corporal who carelessly exposed his head as he spat tobacco juice from his chaw.

It was his last enjoyment in this life. His head crossed the gun sights, exploded like an overripe melon.

The other guns were hammering in a furious volley and the troopers didn't have a chance; their hearts didn't even seem to be in defending themselves. Just war-weary men wanting it all to end one way or another. Bradford stood, levering his hot-barrelled Henry as he raked his cold eyes along the line of sprawled corpses below.

'Well, you found peace now, you sons of bitches,' he said. He grinned at his men. 'Let's go see what was so important in that wagon.'

As Davis had suspected it was guns: new Henrys, Spencer carbines, Colt pistols, and plenty of ammunition.

No wonder the wagon springs were so flattened and it had taken six mules to haul it. There were enough arms here to start the war all over again.

Bradford was almost ready to dance,

grinning widely.

'God*damn*! Didn't I tell you it had to be somethin' good to need a whole blame troop and a lieutenant!'

Davis looked at a case already opened by Matheson. It was crammed with new Henry repeaters, with buffed-iron actions; it was a year away yet from the brass actions that would give the trusty old Henry the nickname of 'Yellowboy'.

Davis hefted it, the legendary rifle which, according to startled Johnny Rebs, gave the Yankees the ability to 'load on Sunday and keep shootin' all week long.'

'Got better balance than the last model,' he opined. 'Sights look more substantial, too. Yours are always bending out of line, Chet.'

Bradford grunted and picked up one of the new long-barrelled rifles, too, put it to his shoulder, sighted along the barrel, worked lever and hammer and trigger. 'Ought to bring a couple hundred *pesos* apiece south of the Rio.'

Silence fell like someone had closed a door in a small room with no windows.

After a breath or two, Davis said slowly: 'That where you're aiming to get rid of 'em?'

'Hell, obvious, ain't it? That foreign duke or whatever he is has Mexico in a fine old mess. Rebels everywhere, payin' top prices for good ol' American guns! Boys, we're rich!'

They must have thought so, too, because they all started yelling and talking at once, young Boone beginning an improvised Indian war dance. Davis smiled slowly, resting the gun he had chosen on the edge of the wagon, opening one of the ammunition boxes. He brought out six cartons of fifty cartridges each. Bradford saw him first and walked across.

'What you got in mind?'

'Need a reliable rifle.'

'For . . . ?'

Davis set his gaze on the man's sweaty face. 'Goin' home.'

Bradford looked relieved, though

19

wary. 'We'll all go home rich after we get back from Mexico.'

'Not me, Chet.'

The others saw Bradford's face and the yelling and laughter subsided. They closed around Davis in a small, tight circle.

'We need you, Link,' Bradford said slowly and, strangely, reluctantly. His eyes were like the bullets at the end of the brass shells Davis was loading into the long, underbarrel magazine. 'You know this country — and you've been to Mexico heaps of times. You told us often enough.'

Davis nodded. 'True. But I ain't taking any guns across the Rio.'

'Judas, man, we can make our fortune here!'

'Like we could've a hundred times since we formed our own band and kicked hell outta the Yanks?' Before Bradford could answer, Davis shook his head. 'We've each had a fortune ten times over, Chet. Blew it all like fools. Well, I'm headed back to the old man's spread in the Big Bend. About all I'm taking is myself and this gun and maybe somewhere along the trail I'll steal myself a decent horse. He needs me, Chet. Ain't heard from him in over a year. He's old, poorly, and I need to go help him out. I can do that now there's peace.'

Matheson spat. 'Peace? You think them damn Yankees are gonna forget what we done to 'em, Davis? I don't mean just us Trail Wolves, but every Johnny Reb who survived and their families. They're gonna whup us good! They beat us and they ain't gonna let us forget we spat in their eye! Take my word for it!'

The others, including Davis, agreed.

'Yeah, like that Major Reece said, there's hard times ahead. That's why I have to be there to help my father. Ain't any of you got kinfolk still surviving?'

They fell silent and Boone said, with a trace of a catch in his voice, 'Had a sister up in Crosskey. I heard she — survived, after a Yankee regiment razed the town. But I dunno if it's true or where she is now.'

No one else answered Davis. He looked around at the hard, dirty, stubbled faces — except for Curly Keller's shiny, cleanshaven one — and nodded. 'Been nice knowin' you, boys. The war didn't do much to make us good men, but we did what we had to. You're ever in the Big Bend, come lookin' for me. The Rollin' D. Ten miles north-west of Cataract.'

He started to turn away towards where their horses were ground-hitched, but Bradford's hand tightened on his left arm. 'Wait up, Link. There's still that trail down into Mexico. You can take time to lead us down safely.'

Davis waited, then said: 'I'll get you started, then draw you a map. Shortest trail I know'll take you into Coahuila. Head south to the hills around Monclova. There's Rebs by the hundreds up there.'

'What makes it so popular?' Keller demanded.

'Was once the capital when Texas and Coahuila were all part of Mexico — some symbolic thing. Feller name of Cortiz, Luiz Cortiz, is sort of head honcho down that way. Just ask around for *El Tigre*.'

'Jesus, these goddamned peasants sure like the fancy names,' opined Bradford.

'"Tiger" is what they call jaguars down there.'

'Jaguars!' exclaimed Boone, looking worried. 'They . . . eat you, don't they?'

'Not if you run fast enough.' Bradford chuckled. 'Or shoot fast enough. Link, how come you know so much about this *bandido*?'

Davis took his time answering. 'Did some business with him couple of times. Freighted in some grub and booze for his men, had to run the gauntlet of *rurales* and government troops. They wanted to starve him out.'

'Then he likes you, huh?'

Davis held up a hand. 'Was a long time ago. I was just a shaver. The Old

Man was more robust in those days. And we needed cash money to buy cattle. Cortiz mightn't even be alive but the Davis name might still count for something.'

Bradford nodded. 'Then I'll use it as a reference.' Which told everyone he had agreed that Davis should draw his maps, or at least set the band on the right trail, before heading for home.

Davis realized it, too, and eased his grip on the rifle with the fully loaded magazine. He could have killed them all if they'd tried to stop him, but he was kind of glad it had worked out this way. Though he knew he might live to regret it. 'I'll ride aways south with you, set you on the right trail before heading west for Texas.'

It was the least he could do. Or the best.

2

West to Texas

They cleared Alabama without sighting any more Yankees — well, not quite. They saw hazy patches lifted at most points of the compass, the unmistakable funnelling of dust from many riders, but they took precautions to give them all a wide berth.

Bradford wasn't all that happy; he still had an itchy trigger finger. Davis saw he was growing restless and laid it on the line:

'Chet, the last thing we need is to tangle with a Yankee troop out hunting down Rebs like us. The wagon's branded 'Union Army' and that'd be enough for them to unlimber their rifles or shake out a loop in a lariat and head for the nearest cottonwood. Forget about any more fighting. You want to go hunting trouble, then I'll leave now. You can follow that map I drew without me holding your hand.'

Bradford's square jaw jutted a little further and his eyes had a touch of that cloud that came across them when his dander was up. 'You said you'd take us to the border, Link. Now, you do just that!'

'I will, if we stick to these back trails and dodge every damn Yankee we see — or even smell.'

'*I'm* still leadin' the Trail Wolves.'

Davis folded his hands on his saddle horn, his gaze unwavering. 'Fine. But I'm not a member any longer. Haven't been since Major Reece was backshot.'

Bradford's face stiffened. He had his rifle across his thighs and his knuckles whitened as he tightened his grip. 'By hell, you take some chances, Link!'

Davis said nothing, waiting.

The others had hauled rein and were hitched around to see what was happening, Boone was handling the wagon because he said he'd worked with mules before. Bradford scowled.

'I could *make* you come all the way.'

Davis's mouth twitched slightly. He shook his head. 'You couldn't do it, Chet. And you know it.'

Bradford's ears darkened and his eyes narrowed to slits. He had been touchy about his leadership for a long time, felt it was being badly dented by Davis right now in front of the others. With a sudden, swift movement, he swung his rifle one-handed, the heavy barrel whipping towards Davis.

The Texan jerked his body back but wasn't quite fast enough. The end of the heavy octagonal barrel caught him on the point of the shoulder, skidded off and clipped the side of his head. His battered Confederate cap with its silver badge of crossed sabres, cracked on the bill and with frayed holes worn in the top from years of sweat and dust, not to mention the gunsmoke of battle, flew like a bird for several feet. He hit the ground at about the same time as the cap, rolled away from his mount's stamping hoofs as it snorted, white-eyed, tossing its head. It was close enough to Bradford to slam into the man's horse and this probably saved Davis. The animal's swinging head collided with Bradford as he started to spur forward and the man lost balance, fell to the dust, losing the rifle. He, too, instinctively rolled as the horses untangled themselves and when he thrust to hands and knees, he found himself face to face with Davis. Davis thrust forward, rammed his head into Bradford's stubbled face. The nose spurted blood and, as Bradford clasped it, howling, Davis was on his feet, driving a boot into the other's side.

Bradford rolled and spun, flung a handful of gravel that made Davis duck although none of it hit him, and then the big leader stepped in swinging. Davis took two jarring blows on the side of his head, stumbled. Bradford was waiting and his hands flashed white like fluttering birds, but landed with the impact of a swung rifle butt.

Davis's boots left the ground and when he sprawled and rolled it was not without a lot of agony. Chet grinned and stomped on his spine, swung a boot at Davis's head. The man caught the boot but his grip wasn't quite right and he was unable to twist and heave simultaneously. But the slight twisting he managed was enough to make Bradford stumble, slipping in the gravel, putting down one hand to steady himself. Davis rolled onto his shoulders and kicked the supporting arm from under Chet. The man's breath gusted as his face hit the dirt. Davis bent both legs and straightened them like a bowstring snapping as it drove the arrow forth. The impact shot up Davis's legs and Bradford skidded, scrabbled to grab something that would slow his progress. Davis straightened slowly, wincing at the pain in his side, and by the time he had his breathing back more or less to normal, Chet Bradford reared up like a man surfacing from underwater, badly in need of air.

He closed without hesitation and Davis back-pedalled, parrying most of the blows. He hooked Bradford's arm, threw it wide, opening the way for a frontal attack. He stepped in fast, stomping one worn boot onto Chet's instep, clamping the yelling, flailing man's foot to the ground.

Davis ripped a barrage of heart-stopping blows up under the ribs, hooked Bradford on the jaw, and drove a straight right into the middle of the blood-streaked face. Then he delivered an uppercut, with a blast of air bursting from his aching lungs.

Bradford straightened and was flung backwards, arms swinging wildly for balance. He skidded a few paces, then a leg collapsed and he went down to one knee. Davis was breathing heavily as he moved in, fists cocked. This time when Chet scooped up gravel, he didn't miss. It stung Davis's face, making him swerve and stumble as he tried to protect his eyes. The Trail Wolves' leader dug in his toes and launched himself from a crouched position. Chet's big arms encircled Davis's hips, his legs driving him forward like a steam-train, carrying Davis over backwards. Keller tried to get his horse out of the way but both crashed against it, locked together. The animal whinnied and reared. The fighters separated, rolling into each other as they struggled to put distance between their bodies and those descending, pawing hoofs. Davis felt the wind of one, and it just clipped his shoulder, knocking him sprawling. He spun, ready to thrust to his feet. Bradford, teeth bared like an animal, roared a curse and lunged with fingers hooked, ready to tear out his opponent's eyes. Davis ducked frantically, kicked Bradford in the knee and the man floundered, face twisted in agony. Davis dragged down a hard breath, ready to finish this once and for all, but froze at the sound of a gun hammer cocking.

Matheson had him covered him with the Hawken. 'Just say the word, Chet, and he's hell-bound!'

Davis's Remington had fallen from his belt holster during the fight. He half-crouched now, hands out from his sides. He didn't take his dark, hunter's eyes off Matheson.

Then, panting heavily, Bradford said: 'Put that away, Matt! This is between him an' me!'

'We don't need him no more, Chet!' Matheson said, watching Davis carefully, finger on the trigger.

'Put the goddamn gun *down*!' Bradford roared and Matheson jumped slightly, frowned, and lowered the hammer. Chet shifted his gaze to the battered Davis. 'You won't change your mind?'

'I'm going home, Chet, and nothing — or no one — is gonna stop me.' It was half-challenge, half-threat.

Bradford scowled briefly, wiping blood still oozing from his nose. 'You an' me've never finished a fight yet, you know? Always somethin' stops us before it's settled.'

Davis spread his hands. 'I got the time . . . '

Bradford's face sobered. For a moment it seemed he would go for his gun, then he shook his head briefly. 'No point. Like Matt says, we got your map. You wanna go to Texas, then damn well go. We can get along without you now.'

Davis mopped his face with a grimy kerchief, looked slowly around at the unreadable faces and settled his gaze on Bradford's bitter countenance. He nodded; it cost nothing to let the man save face a little. 'Say howdy to *El Tigre* for me, Chet.'

Bradford curled a lip, then seemed disturbed by a sudden notion as Davis scooped up his fallen gun and rammed it into his flapless belt holster. He kept his hand on the butt as their bleak gazes clashed. 'Hold up. How we know that map won't send us to hell-an'-gone?'

'Only way to find out is to follow it.'

'By hell! You *do* take some chances!'

'Aw, I dunno. I could kill you and Matheson easy before the others even drew bead on me. But leave it lie, Chet.' He raked his gaze around the tensed men. 'That's it, I guess. I'm quitting the pack. Heading west to Texas. You follow and I'll bury you one by one.' He mounted quickly. 'You'll find your way to Mexico, all right.'

He swung the horse on the last words, set it into the brush which closed behind him in moments.

'We better — or we'll be back for you!' called Bradford, sourly. He spat and looked around at his men. They all looked ready to go after Davis, but Bradford said quietly: 'We know where to find the sonuver if we need to.'

★　★　★

As soon as he crossed the state line into Texas, Davis started to see Yankee patrols everywhere. He dodged three but the fourth one had an extra man he didn't know about. When he diverted to get around the main group he found himself looking down the barrel of a cocked rifle.

There were six men in the patrol, led by a hard-faced sergeant named Daggett. He looked Davis over carefully, taking in the dilapidated grey uniform trousers — Davis had discarded the jacket long ago and wore a patched blue shirt — and his Johnny Reb cap, prized by Yankees as a souvenir. The belt holster on his left hip had the gun in it with the butt facing forward.

'What kinda rig's that, Reb?' Daggett asked.

'My own. Clip on the flap busted so I cut it off. Found I can reach across and draw pretty fast if I have to.'

'Looks like a Remington .44, Sarge,' opined one trooper. 'Our officers carry them.'

Davis met the hard stares and said carefully: 'The man I took it off was dead when I found him; his horse had been shot and had him pinned by the legs. Was at Tallow Farm, Indiana, couple years back, after the big battle.'

Some scoffed but the sergeant stared

in silence a long time. 'Could be — but the Henry looks kinda new.'

Davis took a chance. 'A Major Lyall Reece brought us the news the war was over. He'd been celebrating, wanted to be real friendly, and insisted I take his Henry — said he wouldn't be needing it now and as I had a long ways to go to get home . . . ' He let it hang.

Sergeant Daggett was sceptical. 'Home's where?'

'Place called Harrisville,' Davis lied.

'Where the hell's that?'

'Staked Plains.'

The sergeant surprised Davis by grinning slowly, showing gapped, yellowed teeth. 'You'll love it back there — the Reconstruction's got a big headquarters at Fort Griffin. Hammond Dysart, commandin'. They call him 'Devil' Dysart — but sure not within his hearin'!'

The troop seemed to enjoy the joke. Then a trooper rode in behind Davis and swiftly scooped the cap off his head, whooping, waving the trophy.

'Gimme that!' Davis yelled.

'Think I'll take that Henry, while it's still goin', Texas,' the sergeant said, moving his horse closer.

'Reckon not,' Davis said. The whole troop looked kind of stunned. 'Unless you want it this way!'

During the banter, sure they had Davis right where they wanted him, the troopers had relaxed, some even hooking boots over their saddle horns and rolling cigarettes. None of them was holding a firearm pointed at Davis now.

And none of them had ever seen a rifle whipped up as fast as Davis lifted that Henry. He had been riding with a shell already in the breech, the tube filled with fourteen more, and now the hammer was fully cocked before the barrel swung up and covered the Yankees, caught flatfooted. 'Don't you boys know the war's over?'

The man who had stolen the cap swore and started to bring up his rifle. Davis fired over his head, close enough to make the man duck. He lost balance and slid awkwardly to the ground. There was a fresh load in the Henry's breech before anyone could make a hostile move.

'Gimme back my cap,' Davis ordered.

The Yankee spat some dirt, took off the cap, crushed it between his big hands, then with a look of cocky defiance, hurled it over the edge of the nearby cliff. Davis rammed his horse into him suddenly, slammed him across the head with the rifle barrel and still swung it back before the others had managed to make any hostile moves. Silence fell.

Then Daggett squinted as he slowly lifted his hands. The others followed suit. 'It might've been better for Major Reece to've shot you instead of givin' you that gun! If he did give it you! Reckon all Rebs are liars.'

Davis shrugged, but his hands were firm on the Henry. 'Sarge, I've had me a bellyful of fightin' you Yankees — or anyone else. I'm mighty tired and all I want to do is get back home and see if my pa is still alive. You try to stop me and I'll kill the lot of you. Plenty of ammo in the magazine to do it and give me a handful of shells left over. So, be obligin' and one by one walk to the edge of that there cliff and toss your guns over.'

'Like hell!' growled Daggett and there were plenty of other protests.

Davis shot the sergeant's horse out from under him and when the cursing man climbed up out of the dust, the Johnny Reb said: 'That's the last bullet I spend on good horseflesh. Next one's got someone's name on it.'

They were hostile, but one by one they threw their guns over the edge of the cliff into the gulch far below. No one gave him any trouble.

'I'll remember you, mister!' growled Daggett. 'You got a name?'

Davis ignored him, then keeping them lined up along the clifftop, rode in amongst their mounts and started yelling, triggering three shots, setting the horses to running. He rode after them, firing a shot now and again, driving them five miles from where he had left the patrol. Then he dumped the saddles in a river, scattered the mounts and made for the hills and some backtrails that he knew would lead him eventually to Rolling D.

He knew they would try to follow him after they recovered their guns and mounts, so he took time to cover his tracks well. Likely they would have patrol areas within certain boundaries, so they might not search for him far outside of those limits. Although they might send word to the Reconstruction headquarters to keep an eye out for him, Harrisville was a long way from Cataract in the Big Bend. And they didn't know his name nor that of the ranch.

But to be on the safe side, he slipped into a small river town late at night and stole himself a horse, a dun. He took his own mount with him, turned it loose miles away in the scrub above some small hardrock farms. He also stole a shirt and trousers from the washing-lines of these farms. He rode off, still hatless, dressed in a grey homespun shirt that was too loose on him and a pair of worn and faded denim work-trousers. He hacked at his long hair with his hunting knife and figured now he no longer matched any description that Sergeant Daggett might give. The only item that could cause suspicion if he was stopped by another patrol was the new Henry, but he roughed up its outward appearance so that it looked old and well-used.

Then he followed the river for a long way before striking across the Big Bend and gave Cataract a wide berth. He rode so far north and west that he had almost to double back before he could turn south-east in the direction of Rolling D.

His first sight of the home ranch made him grip the reins tight and he felt his mouth go dry.

It looked derelict. Weed-grown pastures, fences sagging, corrals with fallen posts and poles, shingles missing from the barn's roof, *and* that of the house. There were three sorry-looking horses grazing on a patch of dry grass behind the house. Water in the small dam was well down, its sloping sides showing cracked, grey mud designs. He didn't have field glasses or he would have taken a good long look before riding in. But the only way he was going to find out what awaited him was to go on down there and see for himself.

He held the rifle with its butt on his thigh, his thumb crooked in the hammer spur, eyes roving ahead and to all sides. There was no sign of the dogs although one dried piece of rope curling in the dust and attached to the angled corral post nearest the well might have been where he used to tie up Mustard, the big, shaggy yellow-eyed dog he'd had since childhood.

'Hold it there, mister!'

Damn! He had let his attention wander and he was only a few yards from the house now: he noticed the door was dragging, one hinge having dropped. The shutter on the window to the right of the door was partly propped open and a shotgun barrel pointed in his direction.

'Stop right there!' This time the voice sounded a little panicky and the notion of a nervous finger on a shotgun's trigger did nothing for Davis's peace of mind.

He stopped the dun abruptly, held the rifle out to one side. 'Easy! No trouble!'

'What you doin' here?'

'Looking for Lincoln Davis.'

Silence. Then, 'He ain't here!'

'Where'll I find him?'

More silence before the man asked, 'Who are you?'

'His son.'

He thought he heard a sharply drawn-in breath. Then the word '*Judas!*' hissed out and the shotgun was withdrawn from sight. Davis tensed, getting a good grip on the Henry and bringing it in closer to his body now as the door squeaked, jammed briefly, then showered dust from its planks as someone impatiently shoved it all the way open.

Davis swung the Henry down but didn't fire.

A man came onto the weed-grown stoop, a crutch in his left armpit, his trouser-leg on that side pinned up, empty. He was bearded and tousle-haired, could have been anywhere between twenty and forty years of age, his skin greyish. Wide eyes studied Davis and then the thin lips moved across broken teeth in what was meant to be a smile.

'Link? It's me — Benny Grant. We was neighbours before we went to the war.' He slapped the home-made crutch as Davis worked through his surprise. 'Left part of me behind at Marquis Ridge in Georgia so they sent me home. But wasn't worth comin' back . . . ' He gestured vaguely.

'Benny. Good to see you,' Davis said slowly, still not really recognizing this man as the boyhood friend he used to go fishing and hunting with so many years ago. 'Your folks . . . ?'

Benny leaned heavily on his crutch now and shook his head slowly. 'Gone, Link. Buried 'em up on that knoll between your place and ours . . . ' He ran a tongue across his lips and stared out of those wide, haunted eyes. 'Right alongside your pa.'

3

Violent Crossing

Davis's map, rough, though well-drawn, was easy to follow. Bradford wasn't really surprised because Davis was one of those men who had a built-in sense of direction combined with an ability to sketch and observe detail.

They followed the trails marked, glad of Davis's side notes, which indicated water-holes as well as steepness or slippery gravel underfoot, or a narrowness of the trail that could be dangerous to a heavily laden wagon such as theirs.

It was hard going and young Boone surprised them all with his ability to handle the mules. He talked to them in his Southern drawl in an ordinary voice, pitched at a level that seemed to get the animals' attention. He still used the long whip on their dusty hides, though, but somehow they didn't show much resentment.

'Always knew there was somethin' not quite right with that kid,' Matheson allowed as they sat their mounts at the top of a rise and waited for the wagon to make its slow ascent. 'Now I know. He's half-damn-mule!'

'Whatever it is, he's doin' a good job,' Bradford said, suddenly calling down-slope, 'Hurry it up some, Boone! Want to make it across the mesa before sundown, then it's easy runnin' to the Rio.'

Boone waved, grinned, teeth showing white against his dust-caked face.

'Kid's enjoyin' himself,' Curly Keller growled, sounding envious as he caressed the slight stubble on his jaw,

Chet Bradford answered curtly. 'Wish I had the knack — instead I got to worry about you bunch all the time, losin' sleep, gettin' an upset belly.'

'Price of bein' leader, Chet,' allowed Skene. 'But you take things too damn seriously, at times.'

'Kept you alive,' Bradford said curtly and wheeled his mount, walking it over to the shade of a tree where he took out Davis's map and studied it. He was still sullen after the beating he had taken from Davis. It would be a long time before he forgot that — if he ever did.

'Where's the border?' Matheson asked, riding up.

'A far piece. Windin' trail down to the flats and then we go through a dog-leg cuttin' before we come to the river crossin'. He's got some kinda note here.' The paper was crumpled and sweat-stained from much handling and Bradford turned it this way and that, trying to get the afternoon light falling just right so he could read the cramped words. 'Ah. Looks like it says somethin' about 'good place for . . . ' Can't make out the rest.' Matheson nudged his mount closer and tried his hand at reading. He shrugged.

'I don't read much but can make out 'good place', though. Guess that's the main thing.'

'Yeah, but good place for what? Camp, I s'pose, but the word's all smeared. Anyway, if we're close to the ford, we'll cross over into Mañana Land and camp there. Next part's gonna be tricky, gettin' through all that *bandido* country and up where this *El Tigre*'s s'posed to be.'

About that time they heard the snorting of the first mules, smelled their distinctive odour — different from a sweating horse — and Boone brought the wagon creaking and juddering and swaying up onto the more level ground of the mesa. He hauled rein, wiping one hand across his dust-spattered face. Bradford rode up alongside.

'Keep movin'! I want to cross this mesa by sundown.'

'Hell, Chet. Give the mules a breather!' Boone said. 'I can do with one, too, matter of that.'

'You can take a breather when we cross the Rio and bed down, not before. Now, keep 'em rollin'!'

They had to push it to make it across

the mesa before the sun set, and the light was fading so quickly that Bradford relented. Instead of making the precarious descent down to the dog-leg cutting, he agreed that they should set up camp on the high ground for the night. But he had them awake well before sun-up and by the time breakfast was over, there was still barely enough light to see by.

The descent was a heart-stopper, the trail much steeper and narrower than they had expected. Matheson and Skene rode behind the wagon, with ropes attached to the rear, hauling back with their mounts to slow it down so Boone could better handle it on the bends and the steep drop-offs.

Bradford rode on ahead with Keller and they cut back some of the brush that grew out from the earthen banks, blocking the trail in parts. It was obvious it hadn't been used for years. Davis had warned them it might not even exist now; it was ten years since he and his father had run contraband down this way across the Rio, and border weather had a habit of changing the countryside mighty drastically at times.

It was close to noon by the time they were down on the flat, having been delayed because of one serious hang-up on the next-to-last bend, right above a sheer drop of nearly fifty feet into a stony gulch. A rear wheel had slid over the trail's edge, which gave way and Matheson and Skene were hard-put to hold the wagon from tilting dangerously. The cases of rifles shifted and their weight was pushing out the sideboard of the wagon on the lower side above the drop. There was a lot of shouting and the air blued with blistering, imaginative curses.

It meant unloading some cases to ease the weight, then fixing more ropes and using all the riders' mounts to swing the rear of the wagon back onto the trail. Boone was pale and sweating and stood in the seat as he eased the vehicle forward, ready to leap for his life if necessary. But he manhandled the mules around the next bend and halted while the unloaded cases were restacked. He was shaking badly.

The last descent went smoothly and they stopped for coffee and a full meal before tackling the ride through the dog-leg cutting. It was narrow and the high walls cast heavy shadows, making the cutting gloomy and unattractive. The mules sure didn't like it and Boone resorted to more cussing and whipping than he had used previously.

But the wagon went through, even though it knocked loose some heavy hunks of dirt and rocks on the narrow, ragged bends. The southern opening was in sight, with a glint beyond that could only be the Rio.

'Looks closer than it does on the map,' Bradford said, a trace of worry in his voice.

'Well, Davis might've got the scale wrong,' allowed Matheson, 'but it don't matter much. It must be the right place because we can see the river, right?'

Bradford nodded a mite cautiously. He was a little worried. Up until now the map had been accurate, with estimated distances marked in here and there. Unfortunately there was no distance marked on this part, and Bradford wondered if that was because the Rio was *supposed* to be close enough so that estimating distance wasn't necessary . . . ?

But . . . Negotiating the last part of the cutting had been harder than expected, and he wondered if all those rock-studded slopes might have been the result of some kind of landslip that had happened since Davis had been through here. If so, it could have pushed them much further north than they expected to be.

He had just decided to call a halt here while he rode on ahead to scout, when suddenly Boone, standing in the seat, his voice catching, yelled: 'Judas priest, Chet! *Yankees*!'

Their blood ran cold as they wheeled around to look in the direction where

Boone's whip pointed and the goose-bumps prickled their skins as they saw the blue uniforms of the hated Yankees lining hillocks on both sides of their trail, sunlight glinting from rifles at the ready.

'Stop where you are, you Reb bastards! Or we'll blow you to shreds!'

Boone whipped up the mules instantly, but, suddenly reverting to their legendary cantankerous character, the animals balked, honked and straightened their legs, digging in. Boone whipped them and cussed and although dust lifted in a choking cloud from their hides, flecked with a little blood, the mules refused to budge.

Then in a roar of gunfire Boone, standing in the seat, commenced a brief, macabre dance of death, his body jerking, clothes shredded to rags as blood spurted from a half-dozen bullet holes in his lean body. He pitched over the side and — *then* the mules lunged against their harnesses and the wagon jerked forward, slewing as the team splashed into the shallows, dragging the wagon, straining in panic now. One of the cases slid over the tailgate and burst open.

'Got the sonuvers!' bawled one of the Yankees — Sergeant Daggett, no less — as he waved his smoking pistol. 'Stop that wagon! Those're the Union guns they stole!'

The wagon was half-way across the ford by now. Bullets hammered into the straining, panicked mules and one fell, another bucked frantically, wounded. The others strained and lunged wildly and the wagon tilted, a wheel dropped down a pothole and that was all it took for the whole shebang to crash onto its side. Cases spewed out, splintering or sliding, spilling the Henry repeaters into the muddy shallows — past the mid-line: on the Mexican side, strictly speaking.

But no one paid any attention to the wagon now.

Guns were blasting at the scattering men, too, and Matheson almost dropped his beloved Hawken rifle after shooting a Yankee out of the saddle — *blowing* him out would be more correct as the heavy ball picked up the soldier bodily and slammed him down like a gutted rag-doll a couple of yards away. Matheson fumbled to reload but dropped the powder-horn and the heavy rifle bounced and skidded. Yankee lead ripped across his upper right arm and twisted him violently in the saddle. He groped awkwardly for his big Dragoon pistol, reeled as a second slug chewed up his right thigh. Bleeding, not yet feeling pain, only a burning sensation at the wound sites, he wrenched his racing mount to the left, swinging into the dust cloud raised by Bradford's horse, lead singing around his ears as they raced for the river.

Skene was down on his knees, one hand resting against the ground, the other clawed into his chest which was splashed red with his blood. He coughed and pink sprayed into the air, crimson dripped from his chin. A volley of Yankee bullets knocked him flat and his boots drummed briefly before he was still.

Bradford was still shooting with his Henry. He knocked down a Yankee who rose to one knee so as to bead Curly Keller. Chet clung to his horse as it skidded down into a hollow. He heard bullets singing overhead, levered another shell into the Henry's breech and shot a horse out from under the Yankee sergeant who was riding in recklessly. Daggett sailed over the head of the horse as it went down, hit hard, rolling. He lost his Spencer carbine, but swivelled around on one hip and pawed at his Colt in his holster. He was still fighting it free when Bradford's next shot burned a groove across his temple, knocking him flat. Bright lights exploded like fireworks behind his eyes. He lay there, stunned, blood flooding down his face on one side.

A bullet seared across Bradford's ribs, tearing a gash in his flesh but missing bone. He took a tighter grip on the Henry, concentrated on staying in the saddle, guiding the horse into the Rio now. Water fanned in silver splashes.

Matheson wasn't far behind him and he felt his mount stagger as lead tore across its rump. But the animal kept going and, the throbbing pain from his wounds starting in earnest now, Matheson threw himself forward across the mount's neck and gave it its head.

Curly Keller was unharmed as he bolted for his horse, leapt over the rump and somehow managed to slip into the saddle, groping for the reins. A bullet clipped his ear, taking the lobe clean off and he yelled a blistering curse. In red, instant anger, he hipped in the saddle, oblivious to the risk of being shot down, and emptied his pistol at three Union soldiers running down the slope, guns hammering, as he cut across in front of them.

He didn't even feel the bullet jerk his left arm out from his side as if it had got caught in some invisible wire, but he almost toppled from the saddle. As he pulled himself back he bared his teeth and howled like a wolf baying at the moon; his bullets had found targets.

One Yankee was sprawled on the rise, unmoving. Strangely, a Rebel cap fell off his head and rolled down the slope. Something glinted in the early light. The second trooper was down, holding a boot that had been torn up by a bullet, ragged leather and white bone red with pulsing blood showing plainly. The third Yankee had taken a bullet in the neck. He was sitting there, one hand holding the wound, as blood flooded down his side like a spilled pot of paint. He wouldn't last long, Curly thought, and he spurred after Bradford and Matheson.

'Get them Reb sons of bitches!' Daggett yelled, staggering upright, driven by untapped surges of strength to do his duty. Then he suddenly realized there was only one other of his men still on his feet. He swore and ran, staggering, but he knew he couldn't catch the fugitives before they crossed the Rio into forbidden country.

He wasn't quite brave enough to go after them into Mexico; his troop had been strictly prohibited from crossing the Rio at this time while relations with Mexico were very touchy. The order had come from 'Devil' Dysart himself.

No one in his right mind deliberately went against an order that originated with the Reconstruction's chief administrator for Texas. The man could and did treat his own men as harshly as any Johnny Reb if they breached his strict directives.

But, those guns . . . Shouldn't he make some effort to recover them?

How, for Chrissake? Anyway, he was down on his knees in the shallows now, and feeling mighty poorly.

Panting, sweating, Daggett swayed drunkenly, barely able to hold himself upright. He watched the three wounded Rebs splash into the river and make their way over the ford. All of them floundered into deep water and had to half-swim alongside their straining mounts, clinging to saddle horns or trailing stirrups. They were smart enough to keep the tilted wagon and the thrashing mules between them and Daggett and his lone companion.

As they staggered out onto the opposite bank, the soldier who was afoot fired his Spencer's remaining two shots over the muddy water. The sergeant swore as he saw the splash as one bullet fell short of the bank; the other kicked a little sandy gravel far to the left. He watched, fuming, as Bradford and the others crawled out of range. He called hoarsely, shaking a fist in frustration as waves of dizziness engulfed him: 'You'll be back sometime, Reb! And I'll be waitin'!'

The trio of wounded men gathered up the reins of their drenched mounts and dragged them over the rise out of sight. Beyond, all three flopped down, blood-spattered, in increasing pain, knowing they were lucky to be alive.

'Goddamn Yankees!' panted Keller. 'They's everywhere! Din' anyone tell 'em the war's over!'

'They were waitin' for us,' Bradford said heavily, examining his wound, relieved to find it was only superficial. Matheson jerked his head up at his tone.

'Waitin'?' he echoed hoarsely. 'As in — ambush?'

Curly Keller looked up sharply now. Bradford's face was drawn tight with cold anger. He nodded briefly.

'What else? You hear that sergeant yell 'Them's the guns they stole'? They *knew* we was comin'! Davis sent us along that trail, an' I swear it was his cap fell off that Yank you nailed, Curly, I seen the metal badge on the front, them crossed sabres he took off a dead officer, glintin'.'

Keller pursed his lips thoughtfully and Matheson frowned. 'Yeah, Chet, but why would Davis do that? I mean, I don't like the sonuver, but — well, that ain't his style.'

'Why not? That Yankee patrol was all dug in and waitin'. It wasn't happenstance they were there! You saw yourself the trail hadn't been used in years, so it weren't like it was any regular ambush point the Yankees had been usin' to stop *contrabandistas*. And who shoulda been the only one knew we was comin' this way, apart from us? Davis! But the damn blue boys knew — where an' when!'

Keller shrugged; it didn't really matter to him all that much. He was still alive and, for the present, safe from the Yankees. The hell with anything else; he had no use for Davis, anyway, hadn't had for a long time.

Matheson, though, said tightly: 'Never did much like Davis — never did. I reckon he mighta done it, if the Yankees were pushin' hard enough, just like Chet says.'

Curly frowned, slower on the uptake than the others. 'Looks that way,' he conceded, 'but how'd they get his cap?'

'He likely traded it — with the

deadwood about us — to save his own neck,' Bradford allowed.

Keller shook his head slowly. 'Nah, can't swaller that. Look, I'd just as soon cut Davis's throat myself after what he done to me a long time ago, but I just don't see him tellin' Yankees about us, Chet. He was always a queer cuss about honour and stuff. We might have no use for it, but tough as he is, I don't see him turncoatin'.'

'No? Oh, he's a hard *hombre*, all right, mighty tough. But he's had a bellyful of fightin' for months now. All he wanted to do was get back to that hardrock spread his old man was tryin' to keep goin'. Davis is a loner. He was always sittin' to one side of the rest of us, thinkin' his own thoughts. He wouldn't help bring the guns down to Mexico. Chance to make a lot of money, but he passed it up just so's he could head for home and to hell with the rest of us. Nah. If the Yankees jumped him and started to rough him up, and it was delayin' him, I reckon he'd tell 'em about us just so's he could get on his way.'

Keller was still dubious but hated Davis enough to defer to Bradford's shaky reasoning. 'Anyway, to hell with the bastard! We can still deliver what's left of the guns, can't we? There's enough mules to haul the wagon. Davis ain't in it, so that's more for our share, now Boone an' Skene are gone.'

Bradford nodded, looking back towards the river although it was out of sight behind the rise now, maybe sparing a thought for the two Trail Wolves they had lost in this violent crossing . . . maybe.

'We'll go back across the Rio sometime. I dunno when, 'cause we're gonna be hunted by the Yankees as soon as we show our noses — but — sometime we'll get there. And we know where to find Mr Goddamn Davis. We'll get ourselves patched up, boys, and won't worry no more about it. Because Davis is already dead. Just don't know it yet!'

4

Odd Man Out

The town of Cataract was pretty much the same as Davis remembered it except for all the Union blue uniforms dotted here and there on the streets. He had passed the surging waters of the river that gave the town its name about fifteen minutes earlier and the roar had spooked the dull grey mare he had at the end of the leader rope fixed to the saddle's pommel.

It was still a mite skittish from the rough-work he had done on it and his insides were still sore and felt out of place in his body from the battering the animal had given him. The mare was full of spirit, which was maybe why she wasn't carrying a foal like some of the others he had seen amongst the mustangs when he had chased them into his horse-traps back in the mountains. Any stallion who wanted to take this one would have to measure up and wait until the grey was ready to accept him or he would back off with blood gushing down his hide.

He liked a horse with spirit and was reluctant to offer the mare to Roy Bass, the livery owner. Roy must be into his sixties or early seventies by now; long ago, he had been friendly with Davis's father and Davis had been friends with Roy's two sons, Carl and Emmett.

But he needed money now and he needed it fast, and the mare was his only means of getting some.

'Hey, you! You with the grey! Wait up!'

Davis, letting his thoughts run, hadn't noticed that he was half-way along Main now, a street edged with buildings made of rough-sawn planks, with the occasional adobe. The only brick structure in town was the bank. Now he saw the four Yankee troopers, one a lieutenant, barring his way. He hauled rein on his claybank mount — the one he had stolen while making his way home — and looked down into the unfriendly faces. A few townsfolk paused to watch, no doubt they were surprised to see Davis back; for this was his first visit to Cataract since his return.

'I don't know you,' the officer said, taking a black-covered notebook with pencil attached from his tunic pocket. 'Name?'

'Davis.'

'*Full* name, damnit!'

'That's all anyone calls me. First name's Link, same as my father's, which is why they just use my last name. So they don't get us mixed up.'

''Nother queer Reb way, Lieutenant,' chuckled one of the troopers. They were all armed with repeating rifles and revolvers, and Davis knew this was a town patrol, ready for any kind of trouble. Maybe even *looking* for it.

Well, he didn't want trouble in any shape or form. He readily answered the other questions the officer snapped at him: Age? Where was he from? Which outfit did he fight with? How long had he been in the army? Had he ever been taken prisoner? What was his business in town . . . ? Where was he living . . . ?

Davis lied where he felt it was better to do so and the officer soon filled a page of his notebook. He glanced up, twitched his moustache and pointed with his pencil down the street.

'You'll know the Riverbend Hotel. Report to Captain Shelley there.'

Davis nodded and started to move his mount, but the lieutenant deliberately stepped into the way, his brown eyes hard in his angular face. 'You ever salute an officer in that rag-tag army of yours, Reb?'

'When I was in the army,' Davis said slowly.

'I rate a salute *now*. Do it!'

The troopers were grinning. The folk on the walk seemed tensed. They knew Davis as a man who had been on a short fuse before he went away to war, the starter — and finisher — of many a fight on this very street. So they were surprised when Davis made a languid salute and moved his horse forward, forcing the officer to step hurriedly aside.

'I'll remember you, Davis! Could be we'll be seeing quite a deal of each other.'

Davis didn't look back, rode to the livery and tried to keep his face straight as he was greeted by Roy Bass. He was an old man now, looked older than the number of years he carried, wheezed and hawked a lot, was bony as a chicken.

But he recognized Davis and shook hands readily.

'By God, it's good to see one of our boys come back in one piece!' Bass said, his voice much thinner and quieter than Davis recalled. 'Benny Grant lost a leg. Con Connery left an arm and one eye somewheres up north. Tommy Dall — well, Tommy never was too bright but poor sonuver's like a six-year-old kid now, cryin' all the time, not a mark on him that you can see.' He touched his temple with a gnarled finger. 'Plenty wrong in here, though.' He paused, sighed. 'Then there's those who never come back at all, like Carl and Emmett.'

'Guess I was lucky, Roy.' Davis was uneasy in this town now, where once he had spent as much time as he was able to wangle when his father was running the spread. 'Sorry about the boys. We had us a lot of good times together. Roy, how you like the mare?'

Bass had been eyeing the grey from the moment Davis had ridden through the wide doors. 'Looks skittish, but I can see you've done some work on her — '

'How much, Roy?'

Bass's wrinkled old face straightened. 'Well, now, boy. Cash money is hard to come by these days . . . '

'I've heard. But I need enough to get a headstone.'

The livery man squinted. 'For your

pa, huh? Yeah, sad thing, that. He pined for you, son, specially when he started to lose his strength and couldn't do as much as he wanted round the spread. All our boys'd gone to the war by then, place just . . . went down under him. Was that fact as well as the lung fever that finally took him off. He tried to hold on, wanted to see you one more time . . . '

Davis felt the tightening inside him, nodded curtly and spoke more abruptly than he meant to. 'Benny told me all that. All I can do is see his last resting place is properly marked, Roy. Gimme a double-eagle and I'll call it quits.'

Roy scrubbed a horny hand around his grey-stubbled jaw. 'Well, son, them's Injun rates. I'd never offer a white man that little for a hoss he's lost sweat and hide over.'

'Gimme more if you want,' Davis said, half-smiling.

Bass smiled crookedly. 'Like to. Aw, hell, I guess you'll be needin' vittles and such. Look, I got a small poke of double-eagles I been hoardin'. Carl and Emmett ain't gonna be needin' 'em.' His voice caught a little and he cleared his throat, hawked, before continuing. 'S'pose I give you two eagles? Any more and them blue-britches is gonna ask questions. Us Rebs ain't s'posed to have gold or much hard cash. Ain't s'posed to have *nothin'*, way they see it.'

'Sounds like it's kinda hard living here, Roy.'

'We've had it rough — but not like you boys. We manage. Just step clear of that Lieutenant Castle and Captain Shelley. They's hard men and they don't like Texans. They got their job to do and they do it — hell or high water.'

Davis agreed to the deal, left his own mount for a rub-down, and walked out into the street, making for Danton's general store. The stonemason's yard was behind it, near the river.

As he came back out of the store he heard a now familiar voice say: 'Thought I told you to report to Cap'n Shelley, you damn Reb? Something wrong with your hearing?'

The hard words stopped Davis in his tracks and he turned slowly to face Lieutenant Castle and his three troopers. He wished he hadn't left his guns at home but Benny had told him rebs weren't allowed to go armed. Weren't even supposed to hold any firearms at all without special licence.

'Just on my way to report now, Lieutenant.'

'You're going in the wrong direction.'

'Stopped by the store and the stonemason's on my way.'

Castle, a thin man, not unhandsome, but with hard eyes, was shaking his head even before Davis finished. 'You report to the Cap'n right now — We'll escort you and make sure you do it.'

It went against Davis's grain but he didn't want trouble the moment he stepped into town so he went along with them to the hotel that had been taken over by this branch of the Reconstruction.

Captain Shelley kept him waiting for

fifty minutes, Davis watched by two armed troopers meantime. Then he was shown into the office and Shelley didn't even look up from the paper he was writing on.

'Well?' he barked, muttonchops quivering in a florid face, a little sweat sheening the scalp that could be seen through his thinning red hair.

'Davis. Reporting as ordered by Lieutenant Castle.'

'Sir!'

Davis blinked at the word that seemed to explode into the room, then belatedly added, 'sir' but still the Captain didn't look up.

'You took your damn time! Saw you down in the street with Lieutenant Castle questioning you nigh on half an hour back — what took so long?'

'Had some business to do, an old friend to renew acquaintance with.'

Shelley looked up this time, slowly and rudely took in Davis's slim, weathered frame and face, the hunter's eyes, the thin, unsmiling lips, the jutting, unforgiving square jaw. He sighed, set down his pen and leaned back in his chair.

'So! We have us yet another damn Texan with a chip on his shoulder right here, I believe!'

'Not me, Captain.'

'Yes! You, Davis. I can read a man like any book that was ever printed. You're a hardcase, one of these goddamned arrogant Lone Star hard-cases I've been meeting ever since I was posted here! You're all the same. Trouble-hunters, still fighting the blasted war inside you, figuring you won't knuckle under to anyone wearing the Union blues. Well, I've got news for you, mister!'

'Cap'n, I ain't looking to stir up any trouble. I came back soon as I heard the armistice had been made. All I want now is to try and work my spread back to what it used to be.'

'Which spread?' Shelley asked quickly.

'Rolling D — about ten mi — '

'Yes, I know where it is.' Shelley was

reaching for a ledger, opened it, flicked some pages over and then pinned a line to the page with one thick finger. He raised his gaze to Davis's apprehensive face. 'Out where the high country drops down to the river — we've been interested in that area for some time, Davis. Place that close to the border seems to me to be far too handy for men like yourself — desperate for money, with no regard for the work the Reconstruction's trying to do. You might even be tempted to run a little contraband across to Mexico.'

'I'm no gun-runner, Cap'n. Or any other kind of *contrabandista*. Told you, all I want to do is get my spread up and running.'

'Father died some months back I see.' Shelley was scanning the ledger page. 'Seems he just gave up on the place — grew too old to make runs down to Mexico himself, I expect.'

The cold, adobe-grey eyes bored into Davis and he knew then the man was deliberately trying to provoke him. He made himself get a grip on his rising temper.

'Captain Shelley, I believe I was about fifteen, sixteen years old last time my pa took me down into Mexico. It wasn't a way of life with us. Just if we were short of cash. And we never ran guns.'

He stopped as Shelley smiled and leaned forward. 'Like you are now, eh? Short of cash . . . ?'

'I've just sold a horse I caught and broke in, or partly so. I have enough for what I need for the moment.'

'I'm told you visited the stonemason's.'

'You sure have your finger on things in this town, Cap'n. Yes. I ordered a headstone for my father's grave.'

'While your own belly is empty? Well, I'm impressed despite myself, Davis.' He closed the book abruptly, the sound of the pages meeting like a pistol shot. 'Maybe I was wrong — maybe you're the odd man out. You might — just might — be one of these Lone Star buckaroos — is that the right term I've heard used? Uh-huh. Maybe one who'll co-operate with us . . . if we give you the chance.' He paused to light a cheroot, offered one to Davis who shook his head. 'Don't like Yankee tobacco?'

'Had to learn to do without any kinda tobacco.'

Shelley's face sharpened with interest. 'Why? Supply lines bad? Or were you with one of those damn Reb raider bands?'

'Our supply lines were cut for months at a time. I saw no profit in keeping myself on edge just in the hope some tobacco — or decent food or ammunition — might get through.'

Captain Shelley nodded gently. 'I think you evaded my question and yet answered it unintentionally. You're an interesting man, Davis. I hope you'll be smart and co-operate with my men. Because you'll be seeing a good deal of them.'

'Why's that? I'll only be rebuilding my ranch.'

'We-ell — we have to be sure.' Shelley surprised him by standing and offering him a hand across the cluttered desk. Davis hesitated but gave a perfunctory grip. The Yankee smiled thinly. 'We're all the same now, Davis. Americans. No more Yankee or Johnny Reb. They're just labels, mean nothing any more. We *have* to work together if we're going to get anywhere. I hope you're smart enough to see that, for by God, your townsfolk are as hardheaded as statues!'

'I hear your taxes are mighty rough — on us Southerners, leastways.'

Shelley smiled, shaking his head slowly. 'You sure do have a way of speech all your own down this way! Well, death and taxes, you know. Inevitable. What has to be, has to be.'

He walked to the door with Davis and, as Davis opened it, added flatly: 'And I intend to see that what has to be, *will be*. Good luck, Davis. I may ride out and see your place. Quite soon.'

Davis left with that happy thought ringing in his ears.

★   ★   ★

Even the country looked cowed, he thought, on his ride back to the ranch. Folk on the streets had had that shifty, nervous look that a conquered people have, hoping to avoid all trouble, just eager to go about their own business and put in one more day without crossing swords with the victors.

Now the country seemed — to him, leastways — to have the same kind of look. *Hangdog.* He hadn't noticed on his way in, the grey mare keeping him busy as she fought the leader rope. Now he had time to notice and what he saw put a hollow in the pit of his stomach.

This land had been untouched by battle and war; there had been no military engagements this far south; the Yankees had stayed as far away from Texas as they were able, although there was some activity in the far north, on the state's boundaries. But here, folk had just gone about their business, although the 'business' soon deteriorated into scratching out a bare living for themselves while any beef or produce went to the embattled armies of the Confederacy.

It had long been a tolerably poor kind of place, but a man could always feed himself and family by hunting the wild animals in the brush country or the once-lush farmland along the riverbottoms. Now everything looked grey and desiccated and he knew it wasn't only from the lack of rain.

It was almost as if the Lone Star State had given up, but he knew that that was an unworthy thought. It would take more than the Reconstruction to break the back — and the spirit — of this land and its people. Hell, if ever it *did* submit, it would mean everything he had fought for, everything all those men had died for, would have been in vain.

Suddenly he reined down, topping a

ridge capped with shale, where he had a good view clear across to the river. The Pecos was broad and shallow in the upper reaches but through these foothills it flowed into the Rio in roaring, foaming streams not far from here. He knew this was what Captain Shelley had been talking about when he had said this country was too close to the border for comfort: Yankee comfort. He felt a strange stirring; maybe he had been a damn fool not to go along with Chet Bradford and the others on that gun-running deal. He could have led them to *El Tigre* if he was still alive; got himself a grubstake to return to Rolling D with and really put it back on its feet. Maybe . . .

He had been too eager just to get back, to see his father. And yet he'd had a premonition that the old man was long dead. Which really only made it more imperative for him to return and find out for sure, one way or another.

Now he was regretting his actions. The Trail Wolves ought to be down in

El Tigre's country by now, no doubt spending their pesos on booze and women. And here he was with almost empty pockets, a dead ranch to try and revive — and Benny Grant to look after.

Benny was way down in the dumps. He used to be a bright, eager, almost reckless companion before the war, along with the Bass boys. Now — well, a man wouldn't look at the world too brightly if he had lost a leg, Davis knew that. But it was the contrast, seeing Benny so despondent, that had shaken him. Yet the young man had seemed eager enough to come with him and help trap mustangs in the mountains, had actually surprised Davis by how well he could get about; he had managed to cut saplings for the corrals and gates, hopping expertly with his home-made crutch tucked under his left arm, the stump of leg swinging, sometimes throwing him off balance. But he had refused all help to get back on his feet, swearing at Davis more than once — bitterly, too.

Maybe that was the answer: give Benny something to do, a goal, and it would drag him up out of his grimness. Yeah, and there sure was plenty that needed doing, both around the ranch and in the hills. Grant could still fork a horse, not too well, but OK, and there were mavericks to be rounded up . . .

Davis swung his claybank around and started over the ridge and down the far side, having to concentrate on controlling the animal as some of the splintered shale slid away from under the hoofs.

Yeah, get a herd together, drive them up north where he had heard in town that beef-hungry folk would pay thirty, even fifty bucks, a head. Here, a man would be lucky to bring in five dollars a steer, and then only if the Reconstruction felt like paying up.

The brush-living cattle had been undisturbed for so long with so many Texans away at the war, that they were developing an entirely new breed.

Racked steers with long horns, not too much beef, but a knack of being able to go without water for forty-eight hours or more. Now *that* had to be an asset to any trail driver.

Benny was sitting on the stoop when he rode back into the ranch yard. Davis was surprised to see he had shaved and cut his hair some, even washed his shirt; it was still damp, although he was wearing it. Maybe that stint in the hills gathering mustangs had *really* done some good and lifted him out of himself.

Then he noticed the four horses in the corrals, and his eyebrows twitched in surprise as he dismounted.

'How the hell did they get there?'

Benny grinned from ear to ear. 'I brung 'em. You'd rough-broke 'em enough for me to be able to handle 'em. Figured we might's well use 'em down here, break 'em a mite more to saddle, then we can try 'em on round-up.'

Stepping up beside the one-legged man, Davis smiled. 'Well, that's a mighty good idea, Benny.'

'Din' think I could do it, did you?' Grant's smile was tight at the edges and Davis knew this was no time for platitudes or white lies.

'Wasn't *expecting* you to do it, Benny, but mighty glad you did.' That widened the smile and loosened it up some. 'Was I seeing things or was there a slew of mules or burros on the slopes of that knoll I passed just before the trail fork?'

'Nope, you weren't seein' things. Old muleskinner came through — aw, must be six months or more back now. Lasky, you might remember him? He camped here on his way in to Cataract, left his mules while he went into town. That Lieutenant Castle told him he had to pay head tax on his string if he aimed to work 'em around here. Din' set right with Lasky an' he said he'd rather turn 'em loose into the brush — he couldn't pay anyway.'

'That's what he did? Turned them loose?'

'Yep, all twenty one. Yankees shot him and managed to catch mebbe half a dozen mules, but the rest high-tailed it into the scrub. They don't bother us none an' I was thinkin' about how I could shoot one for meat just before you arrived. They gotta have some use, them dumb animals.'

'I've eaten mule before today — and worse,' admitted Davis. 'But we'll leave 'em be for now. I got us some grub from the general store that'll last a few days or a week if we stretch it some. How about I fetch the sack from my hoss and you stoke up the fire? We'll have us sowbelly and beans — and a cup of real coffee. Must be two years since I tasted genuine coffee.'

They both grinned; it was something to look forward to.

There was a good feeling between them again, like in the old days.

Maybe there was a chance of some kind of a future after all.

5

Texas, Adios

The last of the Trail Wolves had been three days riding into Mexico and their wounds were all giving trouble.

None of them had taken enough time in the first place properly to treat the bullet wounds. After they had tangled with the Yankee patrol their one thought had been to rescue as many guns as they could and get that wagon well and truly down into *Mañana* Land. Out of range of Yankee rifles, anyway.

Streaming blood, rough rags having been used to cover their injuries, the three of them, Bradford, Matheson and Keller, had taken time to study the American bank of that part of the river known as the Rio Bravo, making sure there were no more Yankee reinforcements they didn't know about. But there were only the sprawled bodies; the tough sergeant was nowhere in sight. Bradford reluctantly took a ride over there, rifle at the ready and looked around. Six dead men and a horse with blood coursing down its hind legs, another down and gasping its last in great steam-boiler bellows. But Bradford didn't give it a second glance, took what he thought might be useful from the saddle-bags still remaining, then rode back to where Matheson and Keller were staggering under the weight of a dripping case of rifles, struggling to slide it onto the canted wagon.

'We're safe, but that damn sergeant could bring back another troop and this time they might not stop at their side of the river.'

'Well, get on down and lend a goddamn hand!' gasped Matheson, swaying with fatigue. 'You're off joy-ridin', and me and Curly are bustin' our asses!'

Bradford swore, his wound was throbbing and making him irritable.

But he dismounted and lent a hand.

It was an hour before they had the wagon onto more or less solid ground and Keller climbed into the driving-seat ahead of the others. They glared but he lifted the reins and Matheson and Bradford sorted out the mules, even the wounded one, rigging the harness to suit. Curly flicked wet hides with the long buggy-type whip, lifting sprays of water each time.

The mules were feeling hard done by and did not cooperate, but with Bradford and Matheson hazing them also, with rifle butts and boots, they got the wagon moving across the ford and up the shallow slope of the far bank.

There was still no sign of life on the American side and the trio worked the wagon around through the clump of brush and rakish trees, downtrail then into the hollow beyond.

'We ain't gonna make far before sundown,' Keller said.

'A heap further than we are now,' snapped Bradford, one hand pressing into his side which was bleeding again. 'Keep movin'! We need to put as much distance between us and that damn river as we can.'

It wasn't a happy trio that pushed on into the blistering Mexican sunlight. The arid country, with sparse vegetation giving way to cactus and sotol, was depressing.

Then came the mountains, and the first *bandidos*, a ragged, half-starved band, with a few dirty-looking women and several children. As soon as he saw them Bradford knew they were going to be trouble — a lot of trouble, because they were hungry and they had nothing to lose and would fight to the death. The Trail Wolves fired several warning shots and the group hunted cover, not shooting back.

'I don't reckon they're bandits,' Matheson said. 'They just want grub and whatever else they can steal.'

'That wounded mule's more trouble than it's worth,' Bradford said slowly. 'We'll cut him loose and leave him.'

'That ain't gonna give us enough extra speed to outrun that lot!' Keller pointed out.

'No, but they look hungry enough to stop and eat the damn mule. They're mostly 'breeds, lot of Apache in 'em. They're partial to mule meat even more'n hossflesh.'

The trio had nothing to lose and the luckless mule was bellowing, with a newly busted leg, courtesy of Matheson and a sapling as thick as a man's arm.

The wagon ground its way to the top of the rise, the remaining mules working harder than ever. When Bradford hipped in the saddle to look back down below, he smiled.

'Goddamn, it worked!' he called to the others. 'They must be ravenous! Let's get the hell outta here!'

Keller, his wounds aching now, cussed each time he cracked the whip and it was only because it was down-grade and the weight of the wagon pushed them, that the weary mules moved at all. But, once moving,

Keller whipped them up and the wagon gathered speed and forced them to keep going.

They posted guards, taking turns, all through the night but there was no further sign of the bandits or whoever they were. Still working off Davis's map, Bradford realized they were too far west. Luckily, he found a narrow pass through the low but rugged range that barred their way. Two men appeared on a high ledge and fired two shots each but didn't persevere after Bradford emptied a magazine and sent his bullets rock-chipping and ricocheting all around their position. The trio concluded the men were low on ammunition, conserving what they had. Likely a couple from the original band they had left the mule for. This was really dangerous country now.

'That's gratitude for you!' growled Matheson.

As they made their way more towards the east, consulting Davis's map, they missed a canyon that he had marked and became lost in a grey desert which deteriorated into blinding whiteness towards the heat-pulsing horizon.

'Alkali!' croaked Matheson, for by missing the canyon they had also missed a water-hole.

By noon they knew they couldn't make it across.

'What the hell we gonna do?' demanded Matheson.

Bradford shook his head. 'I ain't about to throw away all them guns! *El Tigre*'ll pay a fortune for 'em.'

'Fine!' croaked Curly Keller, stubble on his jowls now. There wasn't even enough water for his daily shave. 'You can buy yourself a gold-plated head-stone!'

'Curly's right, Chet. What the hell good're the guns now? They might be worth a lot of *dinero* down here but they ain't doin' us any good right now. I say we leave 'em, make a dash with just our mounts and we might stand a chance.'

Keller agreed and Bradford, mouth

tight, glared at them both. 'I — ain't gonna — abandon — them — *guns*! I'll bury 'em if I have to, and you two along with 'em!'

He stopped abruptly, looking past his uneasy companions. They knew Bradford could outdraw and kill them both without missing a breath. Now he stood slowly, shading his eyes.

'Gents! I think I see our salvation!' He pointed and the others, puzzled, stood squinting into the glare. 'See it? That big overhang out there? Gravel and splintered shale — take mebbe an hour's work to collapse it and bury our guns. We can mark it, make it across the badlands, find *El Tigre*, bring him back and get paid for doin' it!'

The idea had its merits but the notion of digging away under that ledge didn't appeal. But Bradford was adamant that that was what they were going to do.

'Hell, it can't be far to *El Tigre's* hangout now!' He shook the crumpled, dirty, stained map. 'Look at it this way:

we cross the desert, and we could be rich by tomorrow!'

'Well, you sure perked up from somewheres!' sneered Keller. 'I can't dig, Chet, not with my arm. I'm plumb tuckered, I swear!'

'We do it!' Bradford said and they knew there was no choice now. 'We bury 'em, then let *El Tigre* dig 'em up later!'

Wearily, despondently, the men moved on.

They had only about half the pile of gun-boxes covered with loose dirt and splintered, rotten shale when they heard horses, the jingle of gut-hook spurs. Turning quickly, they saw sunlight flashing from harness adorned with silver conchas as a band of riders homed-in on them.

'There! Told you we weren't far from *El Tigre!*' Bradford said happily, trying to wipe dust from his eyes which blurred his vision. He waved, then heard Matheson swearing.

'Man, are you blind! They ain't

rebels! Look at their uniforms! Christ almighty! They're Government soldiers!'

As the soldiers reined down, lined up, and pointed their gleaming rifles, clicking the bolts, Curly Keller groaned and sat down, tossing his spade aside. He lifted his hands slowly above his head, saying,

'Give up, boys! That's the only move we can make now! Give up an' hope they don't cut our livers out before sundown! *Or* sun-up!'

★　★　★

At last there seemed to be a glimmer of hope at the far end of a long, long tunnel.

Both Davis and Benny Grant were enthusiastic now, following Davis's idea to brush-pop with the mavericks, brand them with the rusting old Rolling D irons and set them on a trail north. Sedalia seemed to be the place, up there in Missouri, where the beef buyers were congregating.

Some talked about Ellsworth, in Kansas, but Davis had always gotten along pretty well with Missourians and he figured to give it a try.

It was blazing hard work under the hammering Texas sun and Davis knew he was going to have to take time off to break in some spare horses to use in the round up. They were wearing down their small remuda at too fast a rate.

The holding corrals that had taken them a week to set up were becoming crowded with wild-eyed, shaggy brush cattle and Davis feared they might eventually knock the fences down if he didn't get them into some secure pastures. Now *that* would be really hard work. Benny had devised a sort of leather bucket to hold his stump of leg so as to give him more stability in the saddle, slinging his crutch horizontally underneath. Mostly it worked, but sometimes when the mount jerked too suddenly in an attempt to cut off a snorting longhorn, he was unhorsed.

Once the steer ran at him, raking with those stabbing, white, pointed horns, and Davis had rammed his dun into the animal, just avoiding the ripping tips himself. Benny had managed to scramble away but his mount wasn't much good after that: it was too badly spooked.

So Benny toned down some of his enthusiasm. Davis knew Benny had been trying too hard, trying to prove he was as good as he had always been in the saddle when he'd had both his legs. He had held off asking Grant to slow down, telling him he didn't need to prove anything to him, but it was still a touchy subject. The incident with the rampaging maverick did the trick, though, and Benny was more circumspect when he rode at some of these brush-wild cattle afterwards.

The tally grew, despite the delay while Davis broke a few more mustangs to saddle. They were skittish and inexperienced, but with lots of bridle work and a minimum of spurs, he won their confidence and they overcame their reluctance to crash into brush and timber and start the mavericks running.

'Bluebellies up on the ridge again,' Benny said breathlessly after they had run a small bunch into the pasture where they were now holding their growing herd.

Davis glanced idly towards the ridge but didn't actually see the soldiers. They would be there, though: he had spotted them in small groups of twos and threes ever since they had started round-up. 'Likely taking tally,' he allowed.

There had been an incident before that, too. One night they heard horses in the yard, rough voices, and found a group of half a dozen soldiers in from patrol taking over the barn for the night. No permission asked, just a flat statement: they were moving in for the night.

They had whiskey from somewhere, shouted, sang, took pot-shots at the house. Benny cursed, said: 'I wish I had my shotgun right here, 'stead of stashed out on the range!'

'Reckon they're wishing the same thing. This is a test, Benny. See if we have any guns hidden away, start shooting back or threatening them while they make a ruckus.'

'Sly sons of bitches!'

So they had stayed put in the house and the troopers had laughed, called them 'Rebel yeller-bellies,' set fire to the barn and rode on out.

The barn was reduced to ashes but there had been nothing of value left in it anyway.

Now, still watching the ridge where he had seen the spies, Benny said: 'They're gonna hit us, Link. Take my word. They let Chad Theodore round up nigh on five hundred head, busted hisself into a hernia, then moved in and demanded head tax. Forget how much it was but it coulda been just a lousy red cent a steer and he still wouldn't've been able to pay. Which they knew all along. So they took his herd, his whole damn spread!' Benny's face sobered even more. 'Poor Chad. Sent his wife and family on to kin in Tucson, then shot himself.' He spat.

Davis nodded. 'Been thinking about the taxes. We got us almost two hundred head now. I figure the two of us could handle 'em along the trail. Be worth at least five hundred bucks up in Sedalia, maybe more.'

Benny's eyes brightened. 'By hell, yeah! We could do it! But they'll stop us, Link. They don't recognize county lines or nothin'. They'll stop us anywhere along the trail.'

'The known trails, mebbe.'

Grant stiffened. Then he smiled slowly. 'Yeah! Them secret ones our pas used before the war when the big rustler gangs were slaughterin' every trail crew that tried to clear Pecos County! And later we used them same trails to run a little moonshine in from Tennessee and sold it to the river-boats. Judas, Link, it's worth a try!'

'Maybe. Then again, maybe we're too late.'

Benny snapped his gaze to Davis, saw the man was now looking at something behind Grant. Benny twisted awkwardly in the saddle, holding his leg stump firmly in the leather bucket. He swore.

A small group of a dozen Union soldiers was riding in. There was a guidon flying on a pole whose base sat in the stirrup-cup held erect by one man. 'Oh-oh,' Benny said. 'That means Cap'n Shelley's makin' a visit!'

Davis's mouth tightened. 'Well, he warned me he might.'

'What we gonna do, Link?'

'See what he has to say.'

There was no choice. They were unarmed: the guns were hidden not far away in case they should be needed while rounding up the mavericks, but it would be suicide to try to reach them. If they merely rode off they would only be chased and caught, probably shot at. So they waited tensely.

The group arrived in a cloud of dust. Shelley nudged his big sorrel forward, Lieutenant Castle at his side.

'Been busy, I see, Davis,' the captain remarked.

'Working our butts off, Cap'n,' Davis agreed.

'How many head? About two hundred? That what you make it, Lieutnant?'

'Close as damnit, sir,' Castle said with a crooked smile. Davis knew what was coming next.

'Tax on that herd will add considerable to the Reconstruction's coffers,' opined Shelley. 'What is the head tax at this time, Lieutenant?'

'I'd have to look it up to be sure, sir, but I'd reckon . . . aw, round about the dollar mark would be reasonable.'

Davis said nothing, Benny Grant sucked in a sharp breath. Captain Shelley smiled. 'You have two hundred dollars, Davis?'

'Reckon you know the answer to that, Cap'n. Figured to earn some cash with these cows. I could pay *after* I sell 'em.'

That amused the officers and even the troopers chuckled. 'Sell them? Where?' Shelley was toying with him.

'Up north.'

Shelley nodded. 'Of course — hundreds of miles away. And you would, of course, expect me to trust you to return and settle your debt with the Reconstruction?'

Davis's face was sober, his gaze direct. 'I give my word, I keep it.'

'Even to a former enemy?'

'To whoever I give it to.'

Captain Shelley glanced at Castle, shook his head. 'Southern honour, Lieutenant! A prime example. But I don't think I can put my faith in it. No, can't be done, Davis. Besides, the tax has to be collected on the spot. If you don't have it, I'm sorry. We'll just have to confiscate the herd. If they don't bring in enough, we'll have to look to taking over the entire quarter-section.'

'Like hell!' snapped Benny Grant but it was a futile protest. 'Judas, we can't just *give* 'em these cows, Link!'

Davis saw that Castle had made a sign to the troopers and they were now under the cocked rifles of these men. 'Don't have much choice, Benny. But, Cap'n Shelley, a couple of weeks back you asked me to co-operate with the Reconstruction. I said I'd do my best because I've had a gutful of trouble. You let us drive our cows to Sedalia or Ellsworth and sell them, I'll see the head tax is paid in full. *Then* maybe we could start rebuilding, which is what I figure is what the Reconstruction wants. Or should. Be something positive to put in your report to Commander Dysart, show you're making progress with us Johnny Rebs.'

Shelley stared in silence for a time, then nodded gently. 'Nicely put, Davis, but I don't need reminding how such a report would be favourable to myself. But Reconstruction taxes must be collected, at any cost . . . to you Rebs, that is!'

'I . . . think I see what you mean. A few neighbouring quarter-sections can all be tied in together on a single land deed, making a full section. Some of these can be added together, too, and make — someone — a rich man.'

'Careful, Davis!' Captain Shelley warned, eyes narrowed. 'Slander can land you in a whole lot of trouble!'

Wearily, Davis waved a hand. 'All yours, Cap'n. Ben, looks like we go back to hardtack and rough living. I don't think we'll ever satisfy the Reconstruction.'

Shelley's eyes narrowed suspiciously at Davis's apparent easy capitulation. Castle was tensed for trouble. He seemed disappointed that Davis had given in so easily. Benny Grant was disappointed, too, but he knew there was nothing he could do about it now — maybe never.

And he knew Davis wouldn't have made such a move if there was any other way open to him . . .

The bluebellies were in control and it

seemed as if they intended to stay that way, grinding down all southerners under heel.

Shelley glanced at Castle and the lieutenant, watching Davis with his cold eyes, said: 'All right, you men. Start rounding up the cattle. You'll give us a hand, Davis?'

Davis, leaning his hands on the saddle horn, merely shook his head. 'Told you — all yours now, Lieutenant.'

Castle seemed pleased; here was an opening for discipline if ever there was one. But a glance from Shelley froze whatever order he was about to give and his lips thinned out beneath his slim, bristling ginger moustache.

'I think our men can handle that number of cattle, Lieutenant. Feel free to stay on for a few days.' He started to turn his horse, paused, saying casually but with a mildly threatening edge: 'We'll no doubt meet again, Davis.'

'Never doubt it for a minute, Captain.' Davis started to turn his linebacked dun. 'C'mon, Benny. Let's get inside out of the sun and pack our gear.'

As they headed back to the house, they heard the shouts and racing hoofs as the soldiers started to round up the mavericks. Or tried to. They were not very experienced in handling cattle and these were fresh in from the brush, skittish and bad-tempered. Looking back, Benny's face, which had been sullen since they had left the Yankees, suddenly split into a smile.

'Wow-eeee!' he whooped. 'Lookit them bluebellies losin' sweat — and some hide, too, I'm glad to say! Fallin' off their hosses like tin ducks in a shootin' gallery at the funfair!'

'Keep riding, Ben,' Davis said without turning. 'Keep riding. When we get behind that stand of dusty pine, we swing left and cut back through the dry wash.'

Frowning, but keeping his horse moving in the general direction of the distant ranch house, Grant said: 'That'll take us back to the range we just been workin'!'

Davis nodded, adding, quietly: 'And our guns.'

Grant almost hauled rein at the words. 'Hell! Knew you wouldn't give in that easy!'

'Well, I've had enough of fighting, but that don't mean I *won't* fight if I figure I have to.'

'You . . . you ain't gonna take on all them soldiers, Link! Hell almighty, they'll shoot us to shreds!'

'If we stay still long enough for 'em to draw bead. But they're mighty busy right now, their own guns are holstered or strapped down in saddle boots . . . We hit that herd just right, it'll stampede straight back to the hills, scatter to hell an' gone. It'll take 'em weeks to roundup.'

Benny Grant laughed. 'By God, no wonder your Trail Wolves riled them Yankees so much! This the kinda thing you used to do?'

'Anything that'd faze 'em. You game,

Ben? It'll mean abandoning the spread and running for the border. We'll be wanted men and likely won't ever be able to come back north of the Rio. Shelley won't take this lying down but it'll be kind of a . . . last gesture, thumbing our noses at him and all Yankees.'

That sobered Grant and they rode several yards before he replied. 'Years since I been to Mexico. Was thinkin' about goin' down after I come back an' found the spread took over by Yankees. Figured I'd live in your place — till you come back, anyway. Had a notion we could go down there together. Now the time's here to decide and, well, ain't nothin' here for me now 'cept memories — and I can take them with me!'

Davis nodded. 'Yeah. Reconstruction ain't gonna do us Texicans any good that I can see. Mexico's the only place for the likes of us right now.'

In silence then, they swung around the stand of pines, then heeled their mounts to a faster pace, riding towards where they had stashed their weapons.

★ ★ ★

They lay up amongst some boulders at the foot of a tree-covered slope and watched the sweating troopers gradually get the herd into some semblance of order. Captain Shelley and Lieutenant Castle had gone back to town and left a sergeant in charge of driving the herd into Cataract.

'Hell, he dunno spit!' opined Benny Grant gleefully. 'They gonna be here till dark!'

'Suits us better. Herd's gonna be nervous as a new bride cooking supper for her in-laws. Sneeze'll set 'em running.'

'We ain't gonna wait till that sergeant gets a gnat up his snoot, I hope!'

In the deepening shadow, Davis smiled. 'Reckon not, Benny. Let 'em lose a couple gallons more sweat and get the herd all nice and cosy — then just as they settle to supper, we go in a'hellin'.'

Benny Grant chuckled, already strung like a bowstring with nervous tension and rising excitement.

It wasn't quite full dark when they struck.

The soldiers' supper fire was blazing and they could smell beans and sowbelly and the aroma of brewing coffee made them salivate. The troopers were still arguing about who was going to take first nighthawk duty when Davis and Grant burst out of the trees, whooping like whiskey-crazed Indians, their weapons hammering skywards.

The herd hadn't even begun to settle down properly and at the first shot they were up and running. Davis had worked his way around so that they would come up on the herd in such a way that when they ran — away from the gunfire — they would be headed straight for the soldiers' camp.

The troopers took one look at that dark mass spewing out of the gloom, glimpsing rolling eyes and the white flash of clashing horns, snot-dripping nostrils, as bellows like the tormented souls in hell wailed in the night — and ran.

They didn't even run towards the picket-line of horses — army routine had made them follow the usual practice of roping their mounts to a single rope outside the sleeping area. The troopers simply scattered to every point of the compass. Only three managed to snatch up their rifles but they didn't use them. The sergeant drew his revolver as he ran, shooting blindly into the thundering herd. Then he stumbled and wasn't able to get up in time. The rushing longhorns swept over him — and another trooper made the fatal mistake of hesitating, considering going back to help his sergeant. He disappeared under the stomping hoofs, uniform in bloody rags within seconds of his falling. The cattle smashed right through the fire, scattering it, singeing the hides of some animals. The horses reared and whinnied in terror at the picket line. A rope snapped and all but one managed to break free and get away.

Then the remaining men hurled themselves into hollows, behind rocks, tumbling and somersaulting down the slope, anywhere that would take them out of the path of the stampede . . .

The cattle had only one goal: to get back into the thickets they knew, safe from men and their ropes — and guns.

Blowing out his cheeks as he sat his mount close to Davis in the deep shadow of timber, Benny Grant said:

'Reckon we better not hang around here too long, Link.'

Davis nodded, reloading his Remington pistol.

'Reckon not, Benny. Say *adios* to Texas and let's head for the Rio.'

6

Desert Meeting

Thirteen mules.

That was how many they found adrift at the river junction. They looked wary of the horsemen in the early light but a couple honked and Davis knew these were the ones he had seen on the knoll, the last of Lasky's line. Some must have associated riders with Lasky, the man who worked them but fed them also. They took a few tentative steps towards Davis and Grant as the fugitives watered their mounts.

'Guess that stampede spooked 'em outta the hills,' Benny opined and Davis agreed. All the noise, the bawling of cattle, the gunfire, would easily have carried to the knoll which was adjacent to the pasture where the maverick herd had been. Now they were down by the river, cropping grass, not sure where to go next.

'Take 'em with us,' Davis said abruptly, causing Benny's eyebrows to arch almost up to his hairline.

'Them jugheads! Hell, Link, they'll drive us crazy, tryin' to keep 'em together — *and* slow us down!'

'They're used to being together — in Lasky's freight line. They'll stick, but there'll be some frisky ones, I guess. They're worth money to the *rebeldes* for transporting guns and supplies over the terrain where they hang out. There ain't any more rugged in Mexico.'

Benny squinted. 'Well, I never did see myself as a mule-skinner, but if it'll put a few *pesos* in our pockets . . . '

'I didn't say that.'

Benny Grant frowned. 'You just said the mules're worth money to the rebels!'

'Yeah — to *them*. For us, they're a passport. We take 'em in as a gift. Like I said, I don't even know if *El Tigre* is still alive. We'll need something in our favour when we run up against the first look-outs. They won't be friendly.'

Benny nodded now, understanding. 'I savvy. OK. Let's see if we can get 'em across the river, before Shelley sends his soldiers lookin' for us.'

It wasn't easy but the mules, after making token protests, eventually splashed into the shallows and allowed themselves to be driven across into Mexico. There they wanted to browse over the salt-bush and stubble grass and Davis figured there would be trouble trying to move them along until they had at least sampled this food. The mules won that round, so the men hid behind a low rise, ground-hitching the horses, holding their guns, Davis with his Henry repeater, Benny favouring his long-barrelled shotgun. It was mid-morning before they heard the sounds of soldiers on the American bank and they watched through a screen of brush as Lieutenant Castle led a score of mounted soldiers along, looking for tracks. But Davis had covered them easily enough by driving the mules over them, allowing the beasts to tramp around for a spell, muddying the water.

'Somethin' been across here, Lieutenant,' a man in civilian clothes said, the sound carrying easily across the river, sluggish at this spot. He had a Northern accent and carried a Spencer carbine. There was a big-bladed Bowie knife in a sheath dragging at his belt, which was buckled over his shirt that hung outside his buckskin trousers.

'They got themselves a tracker,' Benny allowed quietly.

Davis was straining to hear, tense now, ready to start shooting if need be. Castle examined the churned-up ground, then looked across the river to where the mules were still browsing the salt-bush. He curled a lip and the disdain in his voice was clearly heard by the two Johnny Rebs crouched behind their bushes.

'Christ, man, there's a whole bunch o' mules across there! That's what made this mess.'

'Mebbe,' agreed the scout reluctantly. 'Coulda been used to cover horse sign.'

'Well, friend, my orders are not to cross into Mexico and create an incident that'll bounce all the way back to Washington and then rebound on *me* for disobeying orders! You go across and look around if you want, we'll head on downstream. Oh — and don't expect us to back you up if there's trouble. Shooting a greaser across the Rio's even worse than crossing the river to do it!'

The scout wasn't enthusiastic to go it alone, it seemed, and he shrugged, mounted and rode down the far side after the main troop.

Davis and Benny relaxed, but they were sweating.

Davis spoke quietly, firmly. 'Don't like the look of that scout. He knows what he's about and he could come back. We'll get the mules moving and put the sierras between us and the Rio quick as we can.'

＊　＊　＊

Driving the mules was a pain, just as Benny Grant had predicted. But they persevered and headed south and east through northern Mexico. Both men knew the country from ten years ago, recognized some landmarks, had trouble finding others because of changes through weathering.

But they headed in the general direction of *El Tigre's* country, sweating through the heat-blasted Sierra del Carmen chain down to the Rio Sabinas. After watering, they followed the trail, which led due south towards Monclova and, Davis hoped, to *El Tigre's* band. Skirting the desert that stretched to the horizon, they saw several dust clouds which might have been lifted by riders, but none came in their direction.

They were hungry. Living off this land was not easy, but there were birds here. Benny brought down several bob-whites and Mearns quail but the shotgun had literally blown them apart.

Later, Davis shot a wild turkey, blowing its head clean off, but they were leery about cooking as smells carried far in this burning land of dry air. Cooking could easily bring in predators, two-legged as well as the four-legged kind.

But they had to eat and after they had been travelling for three days, it was their undoing. The turkey, cooking on a spit over a fire that was well hidden from prying eyes caused the upset. The savoury aroma of the bird dripping fat reached out — and brought trouble right into their camp.

The fugitives were hungry, not having stopped to eat since that morning, and then only chewing on cold left-overs. The mules were browsing and the two men had grown used to the animals' honking to each other; they took no special notice of the racket the animals were making. Trail-weary, short of water, too, salivating while they waited impatiently for the turkey to cook, they relaxed and let down their guards.

And suddenly their camp was swarming with riders in the mustard-coloured uniforms of a Government *rurales* patrol. The Mexicans encircled them, gun barrels glistening in the flickering firelight.

'We are just in time for supper, eh, gringos?' He was a grinning soldier with large teeth, a drooping, dusty moustache, and a big pistol that covered them both. Not that it was much of a menace, compared to the other half-dozen soldiers who had them under their bolt-action Mauser rifles.

The grinning soldier didn't take his hard little eyes off them as he spoke rapidly to one of the men nearest him. The man threw a hasty salute, rode off around the rise at the back of the camp.

'Christ, he don't need to send for reinforcements!' whispered Benny.

'Getting an officer. Must be one close by.'

They didn't have long to wait to meet the captain of the troop. He rode in on a big-chested bay, forking an American saddle rather than the big Mexican ones favoured by the soldiers. He wore a dark-green uniform with red-and-gold shoulder-boards, a peaked cap with braid. He rested folded leather-gauntleted hands on his saddle horn, wide shoulders hunching as he leaned forward to study the *americanos*, still seated near the fire, with his bleak, stony eyes.

'Well, I don't believe it! Two Johnny Rebs, caught with grease all over their gapin' mouths! Not even a look-out posted! The Trail Wolves sure as hell taught you better'n that, Davis!'

Davis felt an icy-cold shaft drive through him from the back of his throat clear down to his toes.

The *capitan* was Chet Bradford — and the man who rode up alongside him was Curly Keller, clean-shaven as usual, looking a mite uncomfortable in a lieutenant's uniform.

★   ★   ★

The ropes around his wrists were tightening with every jolting step he took. If he wasn't fast enough he stumbled and fell and then he was dragged for twenty yards or more before Keller slowed enough to put some slack in the long lead rope and allowed him to stumble to his feet again.

'C'mon, Davis!' Keller called back over his left shoulder, grinning. 'You always prided yourself on your runnin' and endurance in the Wolf Pack! How come you can't keep up with this mangy jughead I'm forkin'?'

Davis didn't even try to reply. His throat was drier than the desert sand he staggered over at the end of his rope. There was no longer any spittle forming inside his mouth. The last had dried around his lips in yellowish scum, and was now abrading his sunburned skin.

How much further before Keller called a halt? They had left the rurales' *camp not long after sun-up and it was now well past noon ... How much*

126

longer would his legs hold out? If he fell and didn't manage to get on his feet again, Keller would simply ride on, dragging him along behind. First his clothes would be torn off, and then the desert sand and alkali would begin to rasp the flesh from his bones . . .

He had always known Bradford was a man who never, but never, forgave a hurt, fancied or otherwise. But he had never seen him as sadistic or cold-blooded as this.

And Davis wasn't even guilty as charged! Damn, it hurt, knowing he was going to die, innocent of the betrayal Bradford accused him of: *telling Daggett's patrol the route the Trail Wolves were using to take the guns south.*

'Don't lie to me, you son of a bitch!' Bradford had slapped Davis across the face with a gauntlet, the fingers of which had been loaded with lead shot from shells for Benny's Greener.

Benny had been dead for a hour by that time . . . after the Mexican soldiers had had their fun with him. They made him 'dance' on his one leg, hop around the camp, turn somersaults. Then they gave him his crutch, made him run, and four of them had taken pot-shots until finally a bullet had struck the stick and shattered it. Benny had fallen — and didn't get up. Some of the wild bullets had hit him, too. He was still alive, but suffering. Keller had walked across, looking at Davis as he took his honed razor from the top of his right boot and placed the blade across Benny's throat . . .

'Just like primin' a hog for lunch!' he said — and slashed, jumping back swiftly. 'Man! See him twitch!'

Davis said nothing, but Keller felt a lump knotting in his belly and his heart lurched as he looked into the prisoner's murderous face. He curled a lip and swore, kicking sand at the trussed Davis before turning away with a snarl.

Bradford struck Davis again with the weighted glove, knocking him onto his side. He kicked the downed, dazed man. 'You told them Yankees where we were goin'! They were waitin' for us an' it was only luck we got away! Ah, the hell with this! I don't care whether you admit it or not! I know you done it! And you're gonna die, Davis! But it won't be easy!'

When he was able to, when the torture eased briefly, Davis gasped his explanation in a raspy, barely articulate voice. 'They stole — my — rebel cap. There was a duplicate map in the lining. You were always losing — things — you know that — I made a — second one in case. Yankees must've found — it — set up their ambush . . . '

It had to have been that way — it was the only possible explanation . . .

But Bradford wouldn't listen.

'They caught you! Beat you! All you could think about was gettin' back to that goddamn. hardscrabble spread of yours! So you bought your way out, told 'em where to find us and the guns!'

It was no use and Davis couldn't even speak anyway by that time. They left him while they ate and drank wine and after a while Bradford walked across, staggering a little. He lit a cigarillo, blew acrid smoke into Davis's face.

'What you think of my uniform? Lousy colour but the señoritas seem to like it!' Bradford laughed. 'Better'n Confederate grey, huh? Pay's better, too.' He sniffed, spat. 'Ah. Ain't what we had in mind when we crossed the Rio. Damn Mexes caught us buryin' the guns. I managed to convince the capitan — a *don*, no less: Leon Miguel Uvalde, personal *amigo* of the *Gobernador* of Coahuila . . . I convinced him we were bringing the guns to the governor and that we wanted to join his 'Blessed Army' as he calls it. We said we'd train his men for him in the Yankee way. He liked the idea and gave us all commissions, Matheson, too, only he went to the artillery, showin' 'em how to lay the guns.' He shrugged, bared his teeth. 'Turned out to be a good move, I s'pose. We live pretty good and are pilin' up the *pesos*. Anyway, as they say, it's a livin'.'

Davis stared up but said nothing: he couldn't. Bradford chose to take it as some kind of dumb insolence and kicked him hard in the side, beat him across the head with his loaded gauntlet. 'Sleep well, you traitorous bastard! By mornin' I'll have figured out some way to kill you that'll make you beg for mercy before you croak!'

★ ★ ★

And here he was; being dragged out into the desert, without arms or food or water — why waste such things on a man who was as good as dead? — stumbling through the heat and dust and choking alkali, already half-dead. Not to mention the battering his aching, throbbing body was taking as it twisted and turned and jolted at the end of the rope.

And the man who was causing him this pain was the one he wanted to kill more than anyone he had ever known. Curly Keller: clean-shaven executioner, who thought nothing of cutting the throat of a helpless, dying man, not for any reason of compassion, but simply to watch the pain and horror reflected in Davis's eyes as Benny Grant convulsed.

Well, if Davis was going to die — and that was a certain thing — his last act in this life would be to kill Keller — somehow. And there was only one chance. Only one way his fevered brain could think of.

One chance and if it failed — well, it wouldn't matter too much. He was as good as dead now. It would be better to go down fighting, though, trying to square things for Benny. Maybe one day someone would find his bones out here, but that wouldn't matter, either: *he* wouldn't know anything about it. But if only he could work this! It would be almost a pleasure then to let Nature finish him off — as long as he knew he had nailed Keller first . . .

Not sure where the energy came

from, he abruptly put on a desperate spurt, just for a few feet so that momentarily he gained a little slack in the rope. Enough to grip between his numbed, swollen fingers. He managed to flip a loop of the slack over his swollen hands, then dug in his heels. The rope snapped taut and Keller swayed in the saddle with the unexpected resistance where the rope ran across his hip to the saddle horn. Swearing, he righted and twisted, grinning crookedly as he saw Davis's rigid figure, boots spraying sand as he strove to keep his legs locked straight, throwing his weight back on the rope.

'The hell you think you're doin'?' Keller was amused, half-laughing as he tightened his grip on the rope and heeled his mount forward.

The idea was the sudden jerk would fling Davis onto his face in the sand and then Keller would spur the horse to speed and drag him for half a mile or so . . .

Except that Davis released the slack

of the rope he was holding and Keller, straining against it, suddenly found no more resistance: he was floundering to stay upright in the saddle. Instinctively, he hauled rein, too, and the horse slowed, and Keller found himself falling. He managed to grab the horn and stopped himself half-way, hanging down one side of the sweating mount. Suddenly, the panting, weaving Davis staggered up to him, flipped a coil of rope around his neck and shoulder, then grabbed him by the right leg, heaving. Davis's fumbling fingers grabbed the razor that Keller kept in his boot-top, and even as the man swung a punch, Davis dragged on the rope and flipped the blade free of the ivory handle.

The sun splintered light from the nickel-plate, directly into Keller's bulging eyes. As he suddenly realized what was about to happen, he began to scream, fighting and bucking to pull himself free, but confined by the rope across his neck and shoulder. Davis looked at him calmy, holding the razor awkwardly between his numbed hands, having no feeling in his fingers, just hoping he was gripping it tightly. He managed to force out a few grating words.

'You never even asked his name, you son of a bitch! It was Benny Grant and I grew up with him . . . Now, die!'

Keller tried to grab his pistol as the horse pranced and snorted. Davis struck, felt the honed edge bite into flesh and then the razor jarred from his grip. Keller's cursing died in a wet gurgling sound as Davis fell to his knees and, for a time, there was another sound — like water splashing from a drainpipe.

When he looked up, blinking, he saw Keller's last twitches in a patch of dark sand, the heavy-breathing horse now standing a few yards away, quivering. Davis groped in the red wetness and found the razor. Awkwardly, he wiped it on his trousers, then carefully set it between his booted feet, pressing them together so as to grip the ivory handles firmly. Grunting, he strained forward, got the ropes binding his wrists against the edge of the blade and rubbed them on the honed steel, feeling them part one by one.

In minutes he was free and the blood surging down his arms into his blackened hands sent hot wires through him. He gritted his teeth and threw back his head against the agony.

But it would pass — and *he was free*!

There was an almost-full canteen of water on Keller's patient horse, grub in the saddle-bags.

And a Henry repeating rifle in the saddle scabbard.

What more could a man ask for . . . ?

7

Payback

Bradford was worried as the sun reeled over and slid down towards the western sawteeth of the sierras, emblazoning the sky, backlighting the suspended fine dust, lending a ruby glow to the encampment. *Where was Keller?*

The soldiers were making their cooking-fires, chattering and joking, unshipping the bags of inevitable beans and chilli and the good strong coffee, ready for grinding before brewing. That was one thing these men of his *could* do — make a decent cup of coffee, even out here in this god-forsaken back-lot.

But his mind was on Curly Keller.

And Davis. Keller had been eager to drag Davis out into the desert and leave him to die a lingering death. He had never liked Davis, but mostly he had kept his feelings to himself, though on occasion those feelings had boiled over. Once he had attacked Davis with his razor while shaving.

They had been close to Yankee lines and Keller insisted on making a small fire to heat water for his daily shave. Davis had told him to put it out and when Keller refused, Davis grabbed the man's canteen and used some of the precious water to extinguish the flames. Keller had lunged, slashing murderously with the razor. The blade had sliced through Davis's jacket, opened a gash in his arm. But that was Keller's only victory.

Faster than a striking snake, Davis slammed a fist against Keller's forearm, following through and knocking the man to the ground. Then, before Keller could even try to get back up, lips smashed into his teeth, blood all over his chin, Davis stomped on the hand holding the razor, ground it into the dirt while Keller writhed and swore and yelled. Davis grabbed his ears, banged his head on the ground several times and while the man was dazed picked up the razor, stood on the blade and wrenched the handle up. The shank snapped and he dropped the two pieces on Keller's heaving chest.

The razor had originally belonged to Keller's father.

It was no wonder there had been bad blood between them, but Keller was leery of Davis, biding his time, swore he could wait for the right opportunity to square things . . .

'Well, I hope like hell you did the squarin' and not Davis,' Bradford murmured now as one of the soldiers brought him his first mug of coffee. He sipped the steaming black liquid and sat on the log, waiting for his plate of beans and chilli, staring out into the darkening land.

He was suddenly aware of a hard knot in his belly. He swore under his breath. *Damn Davis! He wouldn't be able to relax until he knew for sure the man was dead!*

The smell of breakfast had wakened him although it seemed only an hour since he had at last dropped off to sleep. He had posted guards, got up out of his blankets several times to check that they were still awake, jumped a dozen times at normal night sounds, heart hammering.

Davis really had him going and the knowledge didn't please him.

Still no sign of Keller. *Something must be wrong!* It wouldn't take Keller all this time to drag a man into the desert and turn him loose. Of course. Keller, on the other hand, wasn't the greatest tracker and had a lousy sense of direction, so there was still a chance that the man had become lost, especially if he had ridden far until the sun was going down and had to find his way back in the dark.

If he saw he couldn't make it before night fell properly, he would camp out, wait until daylight and then continue, able to use landmarks better after sun-up.

Yeah, that's what must've happened! There was just no way Davis could've gotten free and turned the tables.

But when breakfast was over and there was still no sign of Keller, Bradford ordered his men to saddle up: they were going out into the desert to look for the man.

That did not please the Mexicans and one, encouraged by the other more timid men, found enough gall to complain. Bradford slapped him silly with one of his gauntlets, the one with the fingers loaded with buckshot. One thing about working with Mexes: they expected to be bullied and slapped around by their officers.

But it only roused Bradford's anger and he cussed them in both American and Spanish — funny how easily a man picked up the swearing and dirty words first of a new language . . .

'A silver *peso* to the first man who spies *Teniente* Keller!' he said suddenly, his words slowly wiping the sullenness from their dark faces. Their pay was miserable and a *peso* meant a few luxuries for them. A woman. Tequila . . .

But although the men strained their eyes there was no sign of Keller. *Or anyone else!* Bradford breathed to himself, by the time the sun was an hour above the horizon.

They rode into some foothills fringing one part of the desert, thinking Keller might have camped there, taking shelter in a cave where it would be warmer than on the sand or alkali. No sign. Then . . .

The rifle shot crashed like a cannon, blasting back from the narrow walls and every man there, including Bradford, jumped and felt his heart leap into his throat. Dragging his pistol free of the tooled leather holster, Bradford felt sweat rolling down his face and from his hair beneath his officer's cap as he spun his horse, standing in the stirrups, searching for the shooter.

He could see by peripheral vision that one of the soldiers was down, dead, shot through the head. The order to scatter for cover had formed in his brain but remained unspoken as the hidden rifle fired again and another Mexican threw up his arms, rolled back over the rump of his whickering, prancing horse and lay still in the dust.

By then any order was superfluous. The soldiers were running in several directions, all seeking their own cover. Bradford swore, rammed home his big Mexican spurs, raking with the large rowels, and lunged for cover in a crevice, where two others were already cramming in ahead of him.

★　★　★

Up on the ridge, Davis lay stretched out on his belly, the smoking Henry searching for Bradford. He had meant to first pick off the soldiers who had tormented Benny Grant, knowing it would rattle Bradford as they died one by one. And, finally, it would be Bradford's turn . . .

But when he saw the man in his green uniform and cap, forcing his way past the two soldiers who were seeking the same crevice as cover, he couldn't take the chance of losing him in the tangle of dry washes and gulches.

His lead spurted dust from the sandstone, ricocheted with snarling whines, caused one soldier to cover his head with his arms, but didn't bring down either man or horse.

Davis reloaded the tubular magazine hurriedly, rolled over and changed position, taking care not to strike the tube against the rock as it was only tinplate, like the Spencers, on these early models and dented easily, thereby fouling the cartridge feed. He ducked as bullets raked his shelter, showering him with chips and dust. He flopped between two rocks on coarse gravel, twisted, and saw that the other two soldiers had holed up amongst some boulders where brush grew.

Davis fired twice, watched between the leaves, caught the glimpse of yellow cloth and hurriedly got off a third shot. A man howled and his companion panicked, jumped up and ran. Davis's next bullet knocked him down violently.

He turned the rifle back to the crevice where Bradford and the other two Mexicans had disappeared. There was no movement there now. Davis held his fire a moment, then triggered a volley, ricochets whining into the morning, dust and rock chips flying. He heard at least two horses whinnying and stamping in fright but no one appeared to fire back.

Davis, stiff and sore from his ordeal of being dragged for so many miles behind Keller's horse, shifted position again. His left leg suddenly knotted in cramp and he fell, rolling over a low ridge of rock, sliding and slipping down into a narrow space below. Before he could get his breath and scramble to retrieve his Henry, there was a ragged volley from the crevice and lead hammered all round him. He spat as dead twigs erupted into his face and sand stung his ears and neck. Working awkwardly with his cramped leg muscle still knotted like twisted wire rope, he tumbled into another hole and lay there, gritting his teeth as he tried to massage the cramp away.

It took time, but he was in a good position here and would see if any of the trio below made a dash for safety. He knew they would eventually. Mexican soldiers weren't noted for staying in one place for long once it became a target. He refilled the magazine to its top capacity, thumbed an extra cartridge into the breech and squirmed around until he was more or less comfortable. It was very cramped and his elbows tended to hit the coarse rock on either side, but he would be able to lever fairly fast and could keep the rifle sighted on the place where he knew they would have to appear once they had decided to run for it.

Whether Bradford would run with them or try to take advantage of the Mexicans' escape attempt as a diversion remained to be seen. Bradford hadn't lived this long by acting recklessly. And he must realize that he would make a stand-out target in that officer's uniform.

Davis had decided that more than likely, mainly because of this latter reason, Bradford would not run with the Mexicans. He *would* use them as a diversion and while Davis was shooting at them, would attempt to escape by another way if he could find one.

Suddenly there was another intense volley of fire and Davis pressed his body as tightly as possible into the rocks as a hail of lead buzzed and snarled around him. Above the sounds he heard the clatter of hoofs. He elbowed his way forward six inches, bringing his face hard up against the rocks where there was a hole for him to shoot through.

He had guessed wrong!

Chet Bradford hadn't waited; he had ridden out with his men, slightly ahead if anything, using them as a partial screen for his back as they crowded their way through the narrow cleft. They hit the open and stayed in a tight knot, dust swirling around them. Davis lunged upright now, bringing the Henry to his shoulder, firing fast. He blew the Mexican soldier on the right clear out of the saddle and the man hit hard, somersaulted, spun and skidded under the hoofs of his companion's horse. But the other soldier was a quick thinker and jumped the horse over the dead man before his mount's forelegs could become entangled and cause him to fall.

He veered away to the left, crouched low over his racing mount's neck, face buried in the flying mane.

Davis swung the Henry and beaded Bradford, also crouched low over his roan, holding his cap in place with one hand, raking the flanks with his spurs.

Davis took his time. He wanted to make sure of this, finish Bradford once and for all.

He squeezed the trigger just once and

the muzzle blast stirred his tangled hair, the smoke momentarily screening his target. Davis jerked his head to one side, waved a hand to clear the swirling powder smoke, and saw Bradford was down, sprawled awkwardly amongst some rocks, his head down between them, the cap with its braided peak and red seams on the top lying on its side a few feet away from the still body.

The surviving Mexican soldier was lashing his mount mercilessly as he made it into the foothills proper, sunlight flashing from his guthook spur rowels. Davis triggered two shots without really aiming: the man was barely within range by now and was of no danger to him anyway.

He watched the rider disappear from sight, and then came the long climb out of the rock hole he had fallen into, and another, not quite so difficult climb, back up and over the ridge to where he had left Keller's alkali-streaked mount, ground-hitched.

His hands were shaking as he

thumbed his last few shells into the rifle's magazine before stooping to move the large rock he had used to anchor the reins. He swung stiffly into the saddle and, rifle butt resting on one thigh, heeled the mount forward. He had to ride almost around the ridge before he found a negotiable trail and then he cantered the horse down past the bodies of the Mexican soldiers, worked through the narrow cleft and dismounted.

Bradford hadn't moved and Davis was sure the man was dead. But he knew Chet of old and to be on the safe side he cocked the hammer of the Henry and approached cautiously.

But there was no movement and he saw the blood staining one side of the uniform jacket and pooling on the hard ground underneath. No man could lose that amount of blood and still be alive enough to be any kind of a danger to anyone.

But even before he heaved the body over he felt the doubt corkscrewing through his belly. *Something wasn't quite right!*

At the same moment as he realized that this man wasn't wearing the murderous guthook spurs favoured by Bradford, he saw the upturned swarthy face caked with dirt and blood.

It was one of the Mexican soldiers, wearing Bradford's jacket and cap.

Davis turned slowly towards the rocks where the surviving 'Mexican' had disappeared.

'You slimy snake, Chet!' he said aloud. 'You made this poor bastard exchange jackets and caps with you . . . '

And Davis had concentrated on stopping this soldier wearing Bradford's uniform while Chet made his getaway.

★   ★   ★

It was easy to see that Bradford was totally unhurt as he fled through the foothills of the sierras. The man had taken time to cover his tracks, at first

151

hurriedly and not well. But as the first haste died in him, he took more time — and he was as good at hiding his tracks as Davis himself. It had been Davis who had taught Bradford and the other Trail Wolves how to cover tracks thoroughly, yet to leave others that *looked* as if an effort had been made to hide them, but they had been deliberately left sloppy, making a false trail.

Twice Davis fell for it. The first one was a genuine mistake and didn't take him long to realize it. He cursed himself for a fool and while still raging came across another set of tracks which could be false. He checked around, examining them carefully, finding three stones that had been upturned and moved to give the impression of a careless hoof slipping on an angled trail, dislodging the stones and apparently pointing the way. But it wasn't the way. Davis scouted around, widening his circles of search gradually and when he came to a place where he could see far ahead he knew that Bradford had tried to dupe him. And he would have succeeded if Davis had galloped off in the direction of the first planted clue.

The trail going this way could only lead to a broken rim above a canyon that was little more than a hole in the ground — but a deep hole, with neither safe entry or exit.

He had wasted some time making sure but when he was ready to move on, his horse — Keller's mount that had made the journey out into the desert and back — started to protest. Long ago, his father had taught him that when a horse was truly tired and had been pushed hard, the best — and only — thing to do was to let it rest. No sense in riding it into the ground. Contain your own patience for a few hours, let the mount browse on some grass, give it drink out of your hat: it would pay off in the long run. It had always worked, too.

So Davis found some grass and a water-hole, dismounted, loosened the cinch and let the horse browse, and stand belly-deep in the cooling water while it drank.

He dozed, though he kept the Henry across his lap. He had found more ammunition in Keller's saddlebags, some jerky, and one of Keller's old campaign caps, crushed in the bottom. As he was hatless he set the cap on his head and, glancing up at the sun, estimating it was past noon now, he mounted and started away from the water-hole.

He had come a long way and was heading into dangerous *bandido* country now. More alert and tense, he rode with his nerves on edge, yet was still surprised when he rounded a bend on a narrow trail below a broken slope.

A line of five armed men blocked his way. Men in big sombreros, with crossed belts holding extra pistols or knives across their chests, their clothing dusty and worn — and death in their hard little dark eyes as rifles were pointed at him.

'*Buenos dias*,' Davis greeted warily. He knew these were *bandidos*, but believed he was not yet close to *El Tigre's* country. Still, dropping the name might be useful. 'I come to find *El Tigre*.'

They stared back coldly and he picked the one in the middle as the leader, a man with streaks of silver showing in his thick hair above his ears, one of which was mangled, likely the result of some past knife-fight. The man's face was scarred, too, a long purple snake running from under his right eye across his mouth and continuing over his stubbled chin. It gave him a permanent leer. He seemed vaguely familiar.

'Who asks for *El Tigre?*' the man said after a while.

'Link Davis. From Rolling D ranch, near Cataract, Texas. The Tiger may remember me as a *muchacho*. Ten years ago. My father did some business with him.'

The scarred man grunted, and was

about to speak when a voice behind Davis said,

'I am *El Tigre*. *Sí*, I remember you, Davis. I remember how much I hated you and wanted to kill you!'

Davis hipped fast in the saddle, for the voice was that of a woman. A young woman.

8

Tigress

The hideout was on the top of a rugged mountain, not quite high enough to hold a dusting of permanent snow, but higher peaks surrounding it showed glaring white drifts amongst the scattered boulders.

Cold winds scoured this place at times, but there were large caves and sheltered spots between the giant, weathered rocks where the *bandidos* had their camp. There were several women and a handful of children ranging in ages from babes-in-arms to twelve or early teens.

It was not the place Davis remembered from ten years ago — but then, *El Tigre* was not the same person either.

She was Annabella Cortiz, daughter

of the original *El Tigre*. Davis recalled her now, a trifle uneasily: as children they had sometimes played together on his visits. When a little older they ... well, he didn't recall any real enmity between them. Just the opposite, in fact.

She refused to speak to him on the way into the sierras, ordered him to be blindfolded and his weapons to be confiscated. His protests met with silence and rough proddings from rifle barrels on the long, tortuous ride to the hideout.

When they had eventually removed the blindfold and after he could see properly, he reckoned it was more a stronghold than hideout. There were permanent adobe and log shacks, a few lean-tos, storehouses, corrals, covered stables for the bad weather to be expected later in the year: a veritable village. A row of rocks and boulders had obviously been positioned so as to make a sheltering wall from which armed men could control the slopes below. It could be well-defended but there were some vulnerable spots. Of course, he realized that on this visit he was looking at it with the eye of a soldier. The other times he had seen it as a child. Romantic. Exciting. *Among the lawless . . .*

'You're well fortified,' Davis opined, speaking to the man with the silver-streaked hair and the scarred face. He got no reply and then Davis snapped his fingers. 'I know you! *El Cicatriz,* The Scarred One. But they call you 'Chico' for short. You showed me how to throw a knife once.'

The Mexican gave him a sober stare, remained silent for so long that Davis decided the man simply wasn't going to answer. Then he said: 'At the time, I was told to keep you entertained, to keep your mind off the *niña,* Anna. *El Tigre* liked you and your *padre* well enough, but no gringo was good enough for his daughter. You must have sensed that.'

Davis frowned, the beginnings of

apprehension knotting his guts now. 'Hell, we were just kids!'

Chico's dark lips twitched. 'You were sixteen, she a year younger — this country ripens youth fast. *El Solo Niño* — the Little Lonely One we called you.' He snorted. 'But you were not so little and growing fast! *El Tigre* wanted to make sure you did not lose your . . . loneliness with his only child.'

Davis felt himself flushing. *There had been one time at the river when they had stumbled across each other, bathing, startled and awed by their mutual nakedness . . .*

He glanced up to where Annabella was talking with some of her men. Still looking at her, he spoke quietly. 'We met once — by accident — at the river, near the big patch of reeds at the old hideout. We . . . ' He stopped, swallowed. 'Is this why she says she hated me and wanted to kill me?'

'She felt much shame afterwards. Then you rode away and did not return as you promised! I think *this* is why she hated you.'

Davis felt the prick of sweat now. *God!* They had been awkward, inexperienced lovers, just the once, and he had sworn he would return no matter what. Except that things had happened, things beyond his control. First, the Revenue Men — an enemy had revealed the location of his father's still, accused him of selling whiskey to the local Comanche. It wasn't true but the liquor-brewing gear had earned his father a year's jail sentence and young Davis had had to work the ranch alone, with occasional help from neighbours. And when his father had come out of prison with the lung disease, Davis was virtually forced to take charge. His father was too poorly to be of much help. Then war soon followed, with six long years of bloody fighting, and once again everything had changed on his return and memories had faded.

He was suddenly aware that Chico was speaking to him. 'What had happened between you was soon discovered and she was much shamed. *El Tigre* was *mucho enojado* — very angry. Twice, he even sent men to bring back your head . . . '

Davis nodded slowly, his heart pounding now as the old memories stirred unwillingly. There *had* been an unexplained ambush down along the river at the round-up camp. Three Mexicans surged across the shallows, shooting wildly, bringing down a rider, Benny Grant's young cousin, Seth Bass, who had been helping to round up mavericks. He had survived his wounds but — *had Seth been mistaken for young Davis . . . ?*

Another time, three weeks later, there had been trouble on the trail drive, when Link had been bossing the herd for the first time. Drunken renegade Indians had swept in, caused a minor stampede, and during the gunfight three Mexicans had come up behind the Texans, guns blazing.

But the wrangler had spotted them in time and they had been cut down.

Afterwards, the cowboys figured they had been working in with the Indians, sent them in first, to keep the Texans busy while they stole the herd.

But, to Davis, it just didn't fit: *pistoleros* didn't operate that way. And he had recognized two of the dead Mexicans as men he had seen on one of his visits to *El Tigre*. It hadn't meant anything to him, because such men drifted on both sides of the Rio, earned a *peso* wherever and however they could.

'Why did the Tiger want me dead, Chico?' he asked now on the mountain, but already he had guessed the answer.

'There was a *nene*, of course.'

Davis nodded. *Yeah, a baby — it had to be! Hell, what lousy luck!* 'I knew nothing about it, Chico.'

'How could you? You did not return.' It was an accusation.

Davis sighed. 'There were things that had to be done in Texas . . . ' He glanced up the slope, saw Anna looking at him. She did not avert her gaze. It was still unfriendly. 'Maybe I better go make my explanations.'

'*Que tengas suerte, amigo*. I think you will need all the good luck you can get!'

Davis thought so, too. He started up the slope. The girl stood there, dusty, tooled leather half-boots slightly apart, her corduroy trousers tucked into their tops. She wore a concha-studded belt with a single holster, canted to the right on her left hip, the pearl handle of a pistol showing. Davis knew this had been a prized possession of *El Tigre's*. She wore a short dark-green jacket over a loose-fitting grubby white blouse, studded leather wrist cuffs, a quirt dangling from her right hand. Her dark hair, swept to her shoulders, had deep reddish glints in it, a legacy from her mother who had abandoned her to *El Tigre's* care soon after Anna's birth. Her eyes were dark and unfriendly, her small jaw slightly tilted as she watched him climb the slope, her full red lips pulled into a tight line. Davis stopped a few feet away, nodded, smiling tentatively.

'This place has a more permanent look than the old one, Anna.' She said nothing, so he asked: 'What happened to your father?'

'What he expected to happen,' she replied coldly.

'The soldiers — they shot him?'

She nodded very slightly. 'A minor battle that will never make the history books. But it freed a whole village from the yoke of *Gobernador* Benedicto Valdez. My father gave his life for those *peons*! And they will never appreciate it!'

'I'm sorry. I liked your father.'

'He was a good man. He cared for me better than that *puta* of a mother ever could have.' Her eyes snapped at him. 'He was prepared to kill for me!'

'And tried twice,' Davis said quietly, seeing her stiffen, the quirt start to rise, but pause, then drop back. *She knew what he meant.*

'You ran away to war!'

He laughed briefly. 'You make it sound as if it was some kind of escape for me!'

'It was!'

'I knew nothing about any baby, Anna. Just before I joined the Texas Brigade my father was dying. I had to try to run our ranch while caring for him. We'd made no runs to Mexico for years and had no intention of starting them again. Then, after six years of hell, I have to be honest, I barely remembered you ... I don't mean it as an insult, but ...'

She went pale and for a moment he thought she was going to draw her pistol and shoot him. He didn't flinch, although all his instincts urged him to dive for cover. Her eyes flashed as she suddenly cut him across the face with the quirt, then stepped back again swiftly.

He drew his hand away from his cheek, fingertips wet with blood from the newly formed gash. But as he moved towards her Chico's deep voice said: 'I think that is not wise, El Solo!'

The man was covering him with a big Colt Dragoon, the hammer cocked. Other *bandidos* had weapons loosely trained on him. Davis eased up, looked coldly at the girl whose eyes were glistening as she held the quirt now in both hands.

'Feel better?' Davis asked in a cold voice.

Suddenly she smiled, white teeth gleaming. '*Sí¡* I feel *much* better! I have drawn blood. Now we are *lios* — *llano* — *ajustar*! Almost!'

It surprised Davis: that one stroke of the quirt had apparently evened the score as far as she was concerned. *Almost, anyway*. He started to speak, but she turned abruptly and headed across the slope towards the biggest adobe house. Chico said softly,

'You should follow, *niño*.'

Davis frowned at the big Mexican. 'Is she loco?'

The mild amusement faded from Chico's scarred face. 'She is *El Tigre*.

He still lives through her. *El Tigre* was one *duro hombre* but he was just. But she is wise as he was; we follow wherever she leads, see that whatever she wishes is done, even if it is not always . . . good. Go make your peace, Solo Davis. It will be best if you do.'

Davis thought so, too, but approached warily. In a small, arched room, she was waiting at a small table set for two. A fat, pleasant-looking Mexican woman in a bright skirt was waiting with salve for the weal on his cheek.

Anna motioned to a chair opposite, and the servant applied the salve. Then food arrived and she said grace simply and quickly in Spanish. The meat dish was roast peccary with lots of chilli which had him reaching quickly for the terracotta water-jug. She smiled faintly and motioned him to silence when he began to speak. 'Later,' she said quietly.

It was almost an hour before the meal was over.

They went out onto a small patio shaded by a brush roof and the

Mexican woman brought a hand-decorated pot of coffee and two clay mugs. She filled them with the steaming liquid and had started back into the house when four laughing, yelling children came running through the area. There were two chubby girls and two boys, one moonfaced, with puppy-fat body, the other gawky and hawkfaced, but laughing loudest.

'Maria!' Anna called sharply. 'Get your brood away from here! You know better than this!'

The Mexican servant looked instantly worried, lifted her apron in a shooing motion as she ran at the children, calling in rapid Spanish. She glanced apprehensively at Anna.

'*Perdon Usted, Señora!*'

El Tigre waved her away irritably, gave Davis a sober look. 'I do not like rowdy children.'

He nodded, smiling as he watched the young ones carefully just outpace the wheezing Mexican woman, giving her cheek, especially the hawkfaced one with the short hair.

'That one's sassy, but children should grab happiness while they can, I reckon,' he said a little pensively, thinking of his own hard childhood. 'Specially these days.' He turned to the girl. 'I didn't know about the baby, Anna.'

Her eyes studied him carefully across the rim of the cup as she sipped. 'It was a boy. He died after only a few days. The snows came early and he was *prematuro*. Too weak.' She was wistful but he saw the firmness in her jaw, too, and knew she had come to terms with this. '*El Tigre* wanted you dead for having . . . spoiled me. Long ago, he had made arrangements with a mission to care for me, educate and groom me for entrance into Spanish society, as far away as Mexico City. He was incensed that now I could never have such a future. I tried to tell him you did not force me. He banished me from his house for six months, made me live with the women who follow the band:

some are wives, some do it for comfort. Then he relented, said he would send men to tell you what had happened, and if you were honorable you would return to marry me. But you never came! I hated you for your indifference. I was *hurt*, Link! It seemed to me that you had taken advantage of me and like every other gringo I knew, you did not care! I was just some little Mexican whore to laugh about around a camp-fire or over a glass of tequila!'

'Jesus, Anna! It wasn't like that! I'm not like that!'

She lifted a hand as he started to explain. 'I know! But I still have this — anger — with you, you see? The sight of you on the mountain brought it all rushing back.' She smiled crookedly. 'I filled with rage. Then I try to calm myself, think about things on the ride up here. Maybe it is good luck — for you — that I think perhaps that nice boy I knew all those years ago has now become a nice man . . . ?'

He laughed briefly. 'A lot of Yankees

would give you an argument, if I said 'yes' to that! I guess I'm like most men, Anna, nice to some people, bad news for others.'

She was sober now. 'Like the men you killed? The *rurales*? Oh, why are you surprised that I know about this? *El Tigre* still has many eyes in these sierras! You killed five, pursued one man for many miles. A special man, I *think*?'

'Yeah. Feller named Chet Bradford. We were in the war together. There were some stolen guns and he wanted to sell them in Mexico, so I suggested he bring them to *El Tigre*. But he was caught by your Governor Valdez, and turned the guns over to him in exchange for his life. Valdez hired him to train his rurales the American soldiers' way.'

'In . . . artillery, too?' There was a tenseness about her question and, frowning slightly, he nodded.

'Maybe. There's another gringo, named Matheson. He knows the big guns.'

She grimaced. 'Valdez now has cannon. If he brings them here and finds our hideout . . . ' She shrugged, frowning.

'Yeah. This is a good place for defence against foot soldiers, even cavalry, but not against artillery. He finds the right emplacements below and he can sit back and pound your stronghold into dust.'

He saw by her face that he had just told her the very thing she least wanted to hear. She was shaken, but, woman-like, pushed the bad news to the back of her mind to be dealt with later. Then she changed the subject.

'And how are you here, Link? The war has marked you, I see, but is it so terrible in your country that you had to abandon your home and run down here?'

'It's pretty bad, Anna. I did have to run. I killed some Yankees who stole my land, so I can't go back.'

She reached out to touch his hand. 'I am sorry, Link. They say you killed those *rurales* in a very deadly way. You will make a fine addition to our band.' She frowned when he did not answer right away. 'Or do you not wish to stay with us?'

'Well, Anna, when I decided to make a run for it, I figured *El Tigre* might be able to use me, but ... '

She nodded slowly, smiling thinly. 'You mean my father, of course. You think I am not as good a fighter as he?' She laughed shortly. 'Ask Chico — no, he will be biased. As will all my men. Better still, ask *Gobernador* Valdez! He has put a reward of twenty-five thousand *pesos* on my head!'

Davis's glance was sharp, momentarily doubting, but then he could see by her face and the arrogant tilt of her head, hear by her words: she was not lying.

She was actually proud of the bounty, seemingly blind to the risk she must be running. The *peons* who rode with her must be very, very loyal, to her or to the memory of the original *El Tigre*, or they had simply never thought of turning her in for all that money . . .

'Chico watches over me,' she said quietly, reading his thoughts, and, surprised, Davis nodded slowly.

'Well, I had hoped I was finished with fighting — but I guess I'll ride with the new *El Tigre*.'

'*Bueno!*' This time her smile was wide, white and warm. It gave her a strong feline look, eyes slanting and unreadable: just like a cat.

Uncomfortably, he thought you could never totally trust a cat.

Any cat. Puma — tiger — or *tigress*.

9

Night Action

General Almeida was a cold-eyed, round ball of a man who sported a small V-shaped beard on his chin and a fine moustache with waxed ends. His sideburns were carefully combed so as to parallel precisely the waves of his glistening black hair. Even his heavy black eyebrows had been shaped symmetrically. His grey uniform was immaculate, the gold braid on the collar and shoulder-boards glistening, proudly proclaiming its authenticity. His leather belt was dark brown and glistening with dressing and polish, as was the buttoned-down holster that held his revolver.

That was as much as Chet Bradford could see of the general, the rest of him was out of sight below the desk but he knew that that was just as neat as what showed above. He sat on a cushion because he had short legs, and was mighty touchy about that particular feature.

'You have returned alone, *Capitán*.' There was a hint of accusation in the general's quiet voice and his slim fingers, two showing heavy gold rings, toyed with a pen made of polished horn.

'Old enemies, General,' Chet said easily, aware of his dishevelled clothing and overall unkempt appearance. But he had a good story to tell, and he knew he would hold Almeida's attention. 'I'm ashamed to say I fell for an ambush, General. Listened as one Judas spoke to me in a friendly manner, reminiscing, while his men worked into position and then attacked us.'

'How many were these enemies?'

'Eight — ten — mebbe a dozen. Can't be sure. I got my men into a defensive position and we gave a good account of ourselves.'

'But you returned alone!'

Bradford nodded, keeping his face expressionless. 'They had the high ground, General — we had to withdraw.'

'You had to *retreat*!'

'OK, retreat. But they knew the country and they picked us off one by one. We had accounted for half of them but we were forced to scatter. I don't know what happened. I found the bodies of my men much later. But I was kept on the run. I had no ammunition. One man crept into my night camp and we fought hand-to-hand. I strangled him but had to leave him before I could take his weapons . . . '

General Almeida held up a hand, sighing somewhat boredly. He knew Bradford wanted to be thought a hero. 'To cut a long story short, your patrol was wiped out but you managed to escape and get back here to safety.'

The smug little son of a bitch, doing everything but call me yellow! Aloud, Bradford said: 'I have travelled a long way, General. I've been thirsty, starved, walked until my boots are more holes than leather, but I bring some good news.'

The neat eyebrows arched. 'One wonders what such news could be. You have lost an entire patrol, all the weapons, the supplies, the horses — and the men. And yet — you have good news?'

Get ready to wipe that smirk off your prissy little face, you greaser bastard! Bradford nodded several times. He carefully brought his gaze up to meet the general's steely eyes.

'I know where *El Tigre's* hideout is.' *Ah-ha! That brought you upright, didn't it? Bounced like the rubber ball you are!* He didn't give the general a chance to comment, but hurried on: 'I was lost in the sierras for a time but stumbled across a group of *bandidos*. One of them was the man who had led the ambush that killed my men — the Texan rebel called Davis. I hid, but saw the trail they took up to a mountain

179

with higher peaks each side of it — a perfect place for our cannon, and with Teniente Matheson doing the gun-laying, why, I reckon we can wipe them out in less than a day!'

General Almeida studied this *Americano* for a long time, still toying with his horn-handled pen, then said: 'You are sure of this? My cannon are too precious to risk going into the sierras only to fail.'

'They will not fail, *General*! You have my word. And Matheson is an excellent gun-layer. He was in the Confederate Navy, fought aboard the ironclad *Merrimac* in her sea battle with the Yankee *Monitor*. He deserted the Navy and joined our Trail Wolves because there was a better chance of more action. We can wipe out *El Tigre* once and for all, and I would, of course, put in my claim for the twenty-five-thousand-*pesos* bounty on the Tiger's head . . . '

His voice lifted in a query and Almeida's eyes narrowed, his lips thinned a little. 'Of course. You are a true mercenary, *Capitán*. You have no real feel for our cause.'

A little more confident now, Bradford spread his hands, smiled crookedly. 'All to our mutual advantage, *General*!'

'Give me time to think about this,' Almeida said, and Bradford smiled to himself: *little toad was just being stubborn — he knew he couldn't afford to pass up such a chance as this!*

Almeida's face was cold and stiff. He did not care for this gringo or his manner. But he was a good soldier and that was what he needed most right now: the *Gobernador* was riding him hard to clear out these damned *rebeldes* from the hills.

As for the bounty money — well, *arrangements* could be made about that.

A dead man could not claim even a single *peso*, except maybe for two — to leave on his closed eyelids to make sure he was well and truly *muerto*.

El Tigre's scouts brought the news one sundown.

'Almeida moves his *artilleria* into the hills, *El Tigre!*' panted the dust-spattered Mexican, sliding from the saddle of his skidding horse, one hand holding to the bridle in expert manner so that he and the animal halted together in a cloud of dust.

Davis saw the girl's face go pale but she tried to cover it. She succeeded well enough, flicking her eyes briefly to the *Americano* before setting her gaze on the messenger. 'Where are they, Paco?'

'They come through the pass. I thought they were heading straight for this mountain, but . . . ' He frowned and sounded puzzled. 'They veered left, to that one.'

He pointed to the next peak across, one that held permanent snow on the upper slopes, which were high above the stronghold.

'He knows where this place is, Anna.'

She flashed him a cold, almost haughty look. 'Then why does he climb the other mountain?'

Davis pointed vaguely upwards. 'To get his guns above.' He turned to Paco. 'How many guns?'

Paco held up three fingers. 'One to that mountain, the others . . . ' He shrugged. 'They make camp in the foothills of that mountain!' And this time he pointed to the right.

'Crossfire.'

The girl was angry with Davis for his comments and he didn't understand why: someone, it seemed, had to point out the obvious.

'It will take them days to get heavy guns up those slopes,' she said contemptuously. 'We can stop them before they have gone a hundred feet!'

'Be better to let 'em get into position, or nearly so,' Davis told her quietly. 'They'll be exhausted, too tired to set up the guns. Hit 'em then and you'll have a better chance of wiping them out.'

'*Sí¡*' Paco was enthusiastic. He might not have thought of that himself but he immediately saw how it could be done. 'We catch them with flat feet, eh, gringo?'

Davis smiled. 'Flat-footed. Yeah, Paco, that's how it's done.'

Anna studied Davis for a long moment, her face thoughtful. 'That is one gun you talk about. What of the others in the foothills?'

'I can take a party down there after dark, drop a couple of sticks of dynamite down the barrels and you can forget all about 'em.'

'*Aiy-yi-yi!*' cried Paco, grinning evilly, showing gaps in large stained teeth. 'This gringo he thinks good, eh, *Jefe*? We have dynamite. *Boom*! No more cannon!'

'How many men are camped in the foothills?' she asked quietly. Paco shrugged.

'Plenty soldiers.' He held up both hands, fingers erect. 'I count twice all fingers, one more thumb.'

'Twenty-one!' Anna was startled now. 'That is the biggest patrol Almeida has sent in since before my father was killed!'

'The *Americano* leads, the *Capitán*. And there is a second gringo, but he go with the cannon to the other mountain.' He gestured to the first peak he had indicated.

As she looked towards Davis he said: 'Could be Bradford. He got away from me and might've made it back to his post. If he did, the other would be Matheson — the gun-layer. We've got real trouble, Anna.'

'These are our hills! They belong to us. It took them almost twenty years to drive my father out of our other mountains to the south. I will not allow them to drive us out of here!'

'Ah! She have the fire of the first *El Tigre*, eh?' There was pride in Paco's voice and face.

Davis was sober. 'Maybe. But did they ever bring cannon in here before? Or at the old hideout?'

Their silence was answer enough.

'It was Almeida's men who killed my father,' Anna said, her words barely audible. She switched the quirt against her leg and the upper part of her half-boot, slapping harder and harder, lifting dust from the cloth of her trousers, marking the tooled leather boot-top. 'I will fight him to the death!'

Davis sighed. 'Strong sentiments, Anna, and I savvy how you feel, but — ' he spoke to Paco, 'was this Almeida with the soldiers?'

Paco shook his head quickly. 'No! He fights his battles from his office or one of his *haciendas*! He earns his medals by trampling on the bodies of his troops!'

'So, looks like we have Chet Bradford and Matheson as our main adversaries. Revenge is OK, Anna, if you're sure of your target. But, like all battles, sometimes it's better to hit and run. Then you can fight another day — '

'I will not run from such rabble!'

'Run, but on your terms, Anna.

That's how we did it in the Trail Wolves. We'd hit the Yankees when they least expected it, then high-tail it and hide out, let things settle, then strike again. It worked for the last three, four years of the war, and was still working when peace was declared, but we had too few supplies — and men.'

Her quirt continued to slap her leg and her bosom was heaving beneath the not-too-clean white blouse as she set her narrowed gaze on Davis. She did not like his manner.

'You think you can make it work here?'

'Don't see why not.'

'We destroy all the guns tonight!' she said flatly. 'Two raiding parties, one for the camp in the foothills, one for the men with the cannon on the mountain.' She indicated the hill to the left. Her gaze challenged Davis.

Davis scratched at his stubbled jaw. 'Anna, why destroy all the cannon? Dynamite those two in the foothill camp, sure, but why not capture the other, use it yourself?'

He saw at once that she liked the second part of the idea and Paco was almost dancing in his excitement. She frowned.

'Is it possible to actually capture a cannon?'

'Reckon so. We'll have two raiding parties as you suggested — '

'I do not 'suggest', Davis! I give orders!'

He shrugged. 'OK. *I'm* doing the 'suggesting' now and I suggest we send a large raiding party to hit the foothills camp because most of the soldiers are there. At the same time, I'll lead a smaller party to the camp with the other gun on the next-door mountain and we'll try to wipe them out and grab the gun.'

'And ammunition. But 'try', Davis? You are unsure you can do it?' She desperately wanted to put him on the spot.

'I'll try — and it'll be a damn good try, I tell you. But there won't be time for a reconnaissance. We'll have to go down there, take a quick look, then improvise. I'm used to it, Anna. It was the only way the Trail Wolves could operate most of the time. If it can be done, we'll do it. I can't say more than that.'

She wanted it to be so and he knew she was only reluctant to give it her blessing because she was irked at his expertise, felt it was undermining her authority.

'Do you agree, Anna? Or do you have another way of capturing that cannon? It'll be a damn big advantage if you can have your own artillery — and I can show your men how to handle it.'

His approach seemed to please her and she nodded, smiling quickly. 'We will do it! Tonight! If you don't succeed, Link . . . '

'If I see we can't capture the gun, I'll destroy it — or go down fighting.'

'There will be no need for sacrifice!' she said sharply. 'We will bring back the cannon.'

'We? Are you including yourself?'

'Of course. I am *El Tigre*.'

A simple statement and she was doing her best to live up to her name, it seemed.

★   ★   ★

Almeida's Mexicans were over-confident. Either that or they held the *bandidos* in complete contempt.

They had only two guards posted on the two heavy cannon in the foothills camp. The rest of the men — Chico counted a dozen bedrolls — were scattered around the ground; many were snoring, all were asleep. A smaller party must be on the other mountain with the single gun.

The cannons had been dismantled, carried in on the backs of weary burros: the wheels on two burros, the carriages one on each of two others, and the heavy barrels on yet two more luckless burros whose spines must have bent under the weight. These were culverins,

cast in solid brass, handsomely deco-
rated, having originally served on one of
the old treasure galleons from Madrid.
These two had long lain in the weather
as monuments facing across la Plaza
Phillippe in Mexico City. Since the
many revolutions, most of the guns that
had stood as monuments in the cities
had been returned to service and put to
the use they were intended for: the
killing of men. But Chico and his men
were not there to appreciate fine
workmanship.

Chico slid one of his slim, balanced
throwing-knives out of the soft buckskin sheath under his jacket. There was
a whisper in the night, perhaps a brief
blur of something passing and one
sentry was down on his knees, clawing
futilely at the blade protruding from the
centre of his chest. He subsided silently,
but his rifle clattered as he fell.

'Que . . . ?' exclaimed the second
guard, some yards to the left, bringing
his own rifle down off his shoulder.

Before he could work the bolt and

maybe waken one of the sleepers, Chico's second knife whispered through the night and the man fell, dying in silence.

While Chico recovered his knives, only one or two of the sleepers vaguely stirring, three of his men under Paco ran to each cannon and began pushing the fused bundles of dynamite sticks into the muzzles. According to Davis's instructions, a fourth man, holding a stout, straight stick moved swiftly from one cannon to the other, prodding the dynamite bundles well down so they would explode close to the breech.

While he was still ramming down the second bundle, the fuse to the first was lit. The second was soon spluttering and the *bandidos* slid back into the darkness. They waited behind some rocks, eager to see the big explosions and how many of the soldiers were cut down by flying shrapnel.

They were disappointed.

Each bundle of dynamite exploded, all right, but the sound of the explosions was deadened by the inches-thick brass at the reinforced breech. But there were gouts of fire, two metallic *clangs!* one a few seconds behind the other, and the muzzles opened out like blossoming flowers. If they had been iron, the torn metal would have peeled back symmetrically. But being brass and of an old casting, the pieces were flung out, whistling with deadly force through the camp. Two men managed to scream. A third sat up and — literally — lost his head. Chunks of shattered casting thudded against the rocks.

Chico yelled delightedly and began shooting into the startled survivors. His men's guns hammered a split second later and, in the blink of an eye, the Mexican *gobernamental* expedition sent to rout the *bandidos* was destroyed.

★　★　★

The sounds of Chico's success were heard on the other mountain where Davis and Anna and four men were closing in on the Mexican camp there.

She was lying prone beside Davis and he felt her hand squeeze his arm. 'Chico!' she whispered.

'Let's go!' Davis was already scrambling up, moving. 'He's got too damn excited and hit 'em ahead of time!'

Certainly the brief though violent explosions and rattle of gunfire from the neighbouring foothills had stirred the camp. As far as the raiders had been able to make out, there was only one cannon here, already assembled on its carriage, aimed towards the rebel camp on the lower mountain, wheels blocked against the slope of the land. The powder charges, premeasured and sewn into calico 'socks' the same diameter as the gun's barrel, were stacked in a box beside it, the balls pyramided behind one wheel.

Seemed the Mexicans were ready to start bombarding the rebel camp as soon as it was daylight, Davis figured. But now the whole plan had changed because the Mexicans had been awakened by the racket from Chico's raid — and these were well-trained soldiers, not the usual dumb *rurales*, forcibly gathered from the ranks of reluctant *peons*.

Rifles with fixed bayonets had been stacked traditionally in threes, ready to grab, between the rows of bedrolls. The soldiers were spilling out of their blankets now, rifle bolts already working, and Davis dropped flat, bringing Anna down with him as the first volley ripped the night apart. He heard the thuds of heavy bullets striking flesh behind him. One grunt of pain, drowned out quickly by a scream. Someone cursed and the second volley from the soldiers cut down two more raiders.

Davis had pushed Anna into a ditch and rolled away, bringing round his Henry, finding the long barrel clumsy and restricting his movements. The Mausers boomed again and now men were shouting and his nostrils were raw, burning with drifting powder smoke. In an instant he was back in the thick of battle, like he had experienced during the war.

He levered and fired at blurred, crouching figures as they ran across the landscape. Spanish curses filled the night, made way for yet another volley, ragged this time as some of the raiders' bullets found targets. Davis slid on loose gravel, still working his lever. He glimpsed the girl crouched in her ditch, firing the pearl-handled revolver. Her face in the powder flash was concentrated, her eyes narrowed, the set of her shoulders determined.

He yelled at her to get down but by then he had slid past down the slope. He twisted with an effort as he saw two men trying to swing the cannon around to face downslope. He felt his knee crunch and twist as he braced a boot against a solid boulder, and the Henry's cracking rimfire sound rattled through the din. Two of his shots struck sparks from the cannon, making the men drop the carriage they were swinging. One man went down and didn't move, the other spun wildly, regained balance and struggled to drag a pistol from his belt.

A gun blasted so close to Davis's ear that he felt the heat. His head rang wildly, dimming the gunfire. He glimpsed Anna reloading her revolver and she gave him a brief grin. Her bullet had killed the wounded Mexican at the cannon.

Then, as the raiders swept in, and the *rurales'* line broke, Davis whirled towards the sound of hoofs. Two men were mounted and riding across the slope, heading downwards. Three bed-rolls were burning and in their flickering light he recognized the riders.

Chet Bradford and Matheson.

10

Relentless

The sun was burning the land when Matheson, sweating, stopped his stumbling mount on the ridge, keeping close to the trees. He was breathing almost as hard as the horse as he fumbled out his field glasses from the fancy saddle-bag he had appropriated after joining Valdes's army.

As he played with the focus, Bradford led his near exhausted horse over the last ridge of broken rock and let the mount's reins trail as he collapsed against a tree trunk.

He swore — and the obscenities were directed at Davis.

'Son of a bitch always was relentless once he got his teeth into somethin' that really mattered to him!' he said, trying to spit, but his mouth was so dry he managed only little balls like cotton.

'Well, he's still comin',' Matheson said grimly, finely adjusting the focus. 'Must've took some Mex's hoss. Got one of them big fancy greaser saddles. Carryin' his Henry and he's got a belt of rimfires slung across his chest!' Matheson paused and swore softly. 'Got a damn big canteen slung, and a grubsack, too. We ain't gonna shake him, Chet! He's after our blood and he ain't gonna give up till he gets it!'

'Well, he ain't gonna see the colour of mine,' gritted Bradford. He came across and snatched the glasses from Matheson. He adjusted focus swiftly, raked the misty trails far below. 'Yeah, look at the bastard! I've seen him before, trackin' some Yankee he really wanted — same set to the way he's ridin' now. Eyes like a goddamn mountain hawk, stubborn as a starvin' wolf. Yeah, he's gonna keep comin', all right.'

Matheson looked worried but he was a tough man and could quickly adapt to most situations. 'We gotta stop him.'

Bradford snapped his head around. 'You want to let him get within shootin' range?'

Matheson shrugged. 'Rather that than hand-to-hand. I still got my Hawken. It'll reach out way beyond any Henry or Spencer and still have enough punch to knock a hoss tail over tip.'

Bradford curled a lip. 'Now where in hell you gonna find a place to bushwhack a man like Davis? You know what he's like, he can read country from a mile away. Likely already got this ridge in his mind, spotted the best places for ambush. He ain't gonna just ride into your sights, Matt!'

Matheson said nothing but his chipped teeth tugged at his underlip. *Yeah, he knew how hard Davis was to stop — but the fact remained he had to be stopped — somehow.*

'All right. He knows where we'll cross — or thinks he does. But s'pose we let him see one of us — you — just nudge a little outta the trees so's he'll see that we are crossin' where he expects — '

'He sees one of us, he'll want to see the other, too. He's no dummy.'

Matheson lifted a big hand. 'Let him see you, just a glimpse, and you fight the hoss like it's slipped into the open for a moment, act panicked as you try to get it back under cover. He'll think it was accidental and then won't expect to see me show myself as well. I reckon he'll be satisfied that that's where we're crossin'.'

Bradford thought about it, allowed it might work. Davis must be weary now: he'd been trailing them for two days and had made up a lot of distance, which meant to Chet that the man hadn't stopped to sleep or take more than a catnap, anyway. If he actually saw one of them, he'd come in fast, take it for granted the other was there somewhere, too.

'OK. I'm crossin' at the top where he expects us to. Where the hell're you?'

Matheson grinned crookedly. 'I'll be already somewhere over the top, waitin' . . .'

'Hell, he won't ride into that kinda ambush! He'll scout first before sky-linin' himself.'

'That's OK. I'll only be *just* over the crest, lyin' in wait so that while he's scoutin' his way, I'll be right under his feet, almost, and' — he patted the heavy Hawken — 'Mebbe you'd care to make a small bet as to how far he'll be blown back down the slope?'

Bradford, smiling faintly, shook his head. 'Don't think I'll take that bet, Matt!'

★　★　★

Davis was suspicious.

It *looked* like an accidental showing of Bradford, his horse's hind feet slipping on the edge of a narrow trail barely hidden by brush. But was it? His narrowed gaze raked the ridge-top but there was no sign of Matheson. Wait — some brush ahead and to Bradford's left was waving about. No other foliage was in motion so it wasn't caused by a breeze. Another rider's earlier passage, maybe, the branches not quite settled . . . ?

With these two, no risk was worth taking.

Davis heeled the big black mount he had taken from the *rurales'* remuda, still not used to the big armchair-like saddle. But the horse got the message of his worn boot-heels and grunted once as it started straight up the slope again.

If Matheson was up there, watching, he would think Davis had accepted the brief glimpse of Bradford as an accident and was now putting on speed, as they would expect him to do — to try to close the gap and get this over with quickly.

Davis felt the big horse straining, its muscles and tendons rippling under his legs as he urged it on. His gaze was restlessly raking the crest. Bradford had disappeared back into the brush now, waving foliage behind him marking his trail. It was up and over and likely in a hurry, so maybe it *had* just been an accidental showing.

Maybe.

Davis worked his way close to the top. The brush was steady now up there. He kept looking towards the section where he had seen the first branches moving. He could see between the sparse growth now, small boulders, half-buried rocks, the suggestion of an eroded trench . . . A man could lie there in wait with a rifle. And blow the head off any rider topping-out and expecting to have time to drop off the skyline before any bushwhacker could draw a bead.

OK. He had it figured now. He worked the horse close to the brushline and suddenly threw himself sideways out of the saddle. The big risers front and back hindered him somewhat, but he made it and just before he hit he raked the blade foresight of the Henry along the horse's flank. Startled, it whinnied and lunged over the top, crashing through the brush.

The boom of the waiting Hawken

thundered in his ears as he lunged over to one side of the horse as it crashed through the brush. He heard the drumming thrust of the big ball as it passed overhead; Matheson was aiming too high, not finding the rider target he expected.

Then Davis was weaving through the clawing branches. He glimpsed Matheson's hiding-place, marked by the big pall of dense smoke from the black powder-charge. He saw the startled look on Matheson's face, saw the man drop the heavy Hawken and claw at the butt of the pistol rammed in his belt.

Davis crouched, working the lever and trigger of the Henry. Matheson jerked upright as if someone had pulled a wire, his arms flailing, revolver falling from his grip, two slugs caving in his chest. He went down thrashing and Davis dropped to one knee, another cartridge in the breech by now. His eyes raked the brush surrounding the ambush site.

But he was looking in the wrong direction.

Bradford had quit his mount the moment he had crossed the crest, run behind the line of low boulders and come up onto the crest again so that he was above Matheson's hideout — and Davis. But he hadn't had time to lever a shell into the rifle's breech and the clash of the lever warned Davis.

Davis dropped flat as the rifle exploded above him and an instant later he felt the burning impact of lead searing across his head. His vision blurred, he triggered by instinct and his bullet slammed into the rock right in front of Bradford's face, ricocheted and tore the smoking rifle from his grasp. Bradford was numbed and shocked at the same time as the bullet shattered and spread pieces of hot lead across his face. He clawed at his eyes and felt the blood on his cheeks, jaw and nose. He reared back and crashed away in a stumbling run, in the direction he guessed his horse to be.

Davis was reeling, fighting oblivion as blood crawled down his face. He sensed rather than saw Bradford crashing through the brush, and triggered blindly. It was a wild shot but the bullet made a lot of noise tearing through the leaves — enough to keep the panicked Bradford running until he found his horse, threw himself across the saddle, and yelled in the animal's ear.

Bradford fought to sit upright, half-blinded by blood, hearing Davis's rifle crash again. Gripping tightly with his knees and twisting the reins about his hands, Chet Bradford sent his mount tearing down the steep slope.

Above, Davis let the hot rifle fall from his grip, sat down heavily and grabbed at the rocks, digging in with his fingers, trying to make the mountain hold still until, finally, he fell off into a black void.

★   ★   ★

The boy with the hawk-like face was staring down at him with big round eyes.

He frowned and felt the bandage around his head, reached up to touch it with trembling fingers. The kid was still staring at him. 'Why — who're — you?'

'I am Tonio Esposita, *señor*. It is my job to watch you, but now I must go and tell *El Tigre* you are awake.'

'Wait! Where am I?'

But the boy had gone from his field of vision and he struggled, trying to lift his upper body so he could see where he was. His sight wasn't sharp or clear. There seemed to be trails of mist before his eyes, but he made out the damp roof of a cave several feet above. A *cave!* He looked again, saw the ragged arch of the entrance, and sunlight beyond which made him squint. But not before he had glimpsed people moving about and — a cannon; light was reflecting from the dark metal.

It started to come back to him then,

but before he had remembered it all Anna Cortiz came hurrying in, trailed by the *muchacho*. The kid stood by, ragged-edged straw-hat in hand, watching with large eyes as Anna spoke quietly to Davis, gently unwinding the headbandage.

'How long have I been here?' he croaked as she examined the wound.

'A day. Chico found you — and the dead man.'

'Man? Not dead *men*?' She looked at him sharply, shook her head. 'Damn! Bradford's still loose then. I saw the cannon outside.'

'*Sí*. We have moved from the stronghold and we brought it with us.' *Yeah, that made sense. Almeida would send other soldiers when his attack force didn't return.* 'We know many places to hide in these hills. I do not think we will settle so permanently again. It is too risky. We must keep on the move.'

'Sounds like a good idea.' He rubbed at his forehead and, at her questioning glance, told her he had a thundering headache.

'You are a lucky man, Link. The bullet could have taken off the top of your head. You must get better and show us how to use the cannon, eh?'

He nodded gently. 'I'm not really an artillery man, Anna, and it might be a few days before I can do much, the way my eyesight is.'

'It must be tomorrow.' She was emphatic, tensed.

'What's the rush? I still feel like the world's sliding out from under me and — '

'Tomorrow, Link! There were some . . . survivors of our raids. They have been interrogated.' He knew what that meant. Poor bastards! 'I have learned something I needed to know,' she added, her face grim, her eyes glittering.

'What's that?'

She didn't answer immediately, then said quietly, while she gathered up the stained bandages: 'Almeida has a prisoner, a very important prisoner. We have been trying to find out where he is being kept — and now we know.'

'What makes this prisoner so important. Anna?'

She turned to Tonio who had been standing by silently, his big eyes watching Davis and the girl closely. She handed him the used bandages and wads of cloth she had used to cleanse the wound, telling him to take them away and burn them. The boy hesitated, but she took him by his thin shoulders, turned him towards the cave entrance and slapped him on his narrow little backside. '*Ahora!*' she snapped and the boy ran out.

'I think he got the message: you don't want him to hear whatever you're going to tell me.'

She nodded solemnly. 'This man, Vincente Esposita — '

'The boy's father?'

She stiffened. 'How d'you know this thing?'

'He told me his name was Tonio

Esposita.' She nodded and he went on: 'Is the prisoner Maria's husband then?'

'Maria?' She was genuinely surprised.

'Yes. When you chased the kids away at the hideout you told Maria to keep 'her brood' away from the patio . . . '

'Oh! The three other children were hers. I just included Tonio at the time. No, she is not his mother.'

Not that it mattered, anyway, Davis thought, *But she seemed more than a trifle diverted by the exchange . . .*

'Vincente Esposita was once a — a — *senalizar?* I do not know your word. He used to send words over the wires — the *telegrafo* . . . '

'A signaller? He worked a telegraph key?'

'*Síj Síj* A signaller!' She paused as if placing the word in her memory for future reference. 'He was in the army but his family was wiped out by Valdes's *asesinos*: his special killer squad. Vincente deserted, tried to kill him but only wounded him and then he was forced to run. He came to us and we welcomed him. On one raid with us, there was a telegraph station and he got some — *instrumentos* — something that he could clip onto the wires and read the army signals.'

'A Morse key. It can pick up the message through the wire so he's able to read the dots and dashes,' Davis explained.

She nodded, obviously not interested in details. 'He has used this a lot, learned much information and was able to warn us when Valdez was planning to raid us.'

Davis nodded. 'I can see how he would be important. To Valdez, too: he'd realize Esposita knows your hideouts and trails. How long has he been a prisoner?'

'Perhaps four weeks.'

'Wonder they haven't put him in front of a firing-squad long before this.'

Her face was pale and very tight now. 'That is what awaits him. He has resisted their torture all this time. Now, according to the *rurale* from the cannon troop, he is to be executed at dawn, day after tomorrow, so . . . '

'So you aim to try and rescue him tomorrow,' Davis said, blowing out his cheeks. 'I can see your hurry, Anna, but I don't know if I'm up to this. I'll do what I can, but . . . how far do you have to drag the gun?'

She gestured vaguely to the mouth of the cave. 'Over one more mountain. The prison where Vincente is being held is on the far side. We did not realize how close we were . . . '

'Well, we both have a mighty big job in front of us.'

'I know where Vincente is being held. You will shoot all round this place and we will release him after the bombardment.'

Slowly, Davis shook his head. 'Anna, I need to see the cannon, check the ammunition — and I never was an artilleryman. It's a long time since I trained and fired a cannon. What will the distance be? Are there walls to be knocked down first? How many guards? I have to know these things.'

'You will have all day tomorrow! Till sundown.'

He frowned, feeling the tautening muscles pull his scalp around the bullet crease. 'Just when are you aiming to make the raid?'

'We must attack tomorrow night Vincente will be executed at sunrise the next morning.'

Davis slumped. 'Moving the cannon over a mountain in the dark is a helluva chore! And there's a big difference between a daytime attack and one at night. The biggest question is vision and range: I have to see the target and drop shots all around it so I don't kill Esposita. Hell, it'd be hard enough in daylight, but at night . . . '

'There will be lights! Why do you look for so many difficulties?' She almost stamped her foot, very agitated.

'I'm not looking for 'em — they're already there. What I'm looking for is a way to overcome them. And right now

I'm damned if I feel I'll be able to do it.'

Her face was white now, her dark lipline contrasting with the alabaster flesh, her eyes flashing, her nostrils pinched. 'You must do this, Davis! You *must*! If you cannot — *will* not help me, then ... ' She drew her pearl-handled pistol and cocked the hammer in a smooth motion, pointing the gun at his head. 'Then I have no more use for you!'

He flinched as the cold ring of the gun muzzle pressed between his eyes.

11

The Battle of El Carcel

They lost a man moving the cannon up the dark mountain.

On the outside of the cannon as they rounded a sharp bend in a steep trail, the rebel strained at the spokes of the big carriage wheel. Then his sandal strap broke and his foot found a crumbling edge of the trail and he slipped. He cried out, hanging on desperately to the spokes, legs kicking in space as he called for help.

Chico forced his pale horse through the throng of men who started to rush to the edge of the trail. 'Keep the gun moving! *Apurate! Ahora!*' He lashed with a quirt across the ragged backs of the men. '*Ahora!*' Chico snapped again.

Used to his commanding voice they set their shoulders to the cannon. The wheel turned slowly. The dangling man's hands slid down the spokes. His fingers were crushed and his frantic pleas were cut off abruptly as he plummeted down into the darkness with a dying wail.

'You could've saved that poor devil,' Davis snapped.

Chico shrugged. 'Maybe. At a cost of time, *señor*. That we can not afford . . . Now you keep moving, *por favor*.'

It was a hard, dangerous chore, this moving the cannon at night over what amounted to little more than a mountain-goat's trail. But Chico drove with words and quirt, Anna raged at the men, alternating this with smiles of encouragement. Strange woman, Davis allowed. Volatile. Swinging back and forth between friendliness and sudden anger.

She seemed very edgy about it all and it wasn't just because they might not find this Esposita still alive. There was something much more personal there, he felt.

Oh, and what was this slight tightening of his belly? Surely not a touch of jealousy?

His head was still a-buzz with noises and the occasional flash of light behind his eyes, a feeling as if all the blood in his body was draining out of him at once. But, as Anna had said, he was lucky to be alive.

Question now was: for how much longer? Because he did not hold out a lot of hope for the success of this raid: it would be almost daylight before they crossed this mountain. He could see that nothing would deter *El Tigre* and that meant he would have to go along with it, even though there hadn't been a lot he could teach the rebels; mostly it was a matter of training them to coordinate their movements.

He was no expert artillery man like Matheson, but he could lay up a cannon OK, was a good judge of distance and wind. If they kept the ammunition coming and with a bit of luck — a lot of luck! — he might just be able to lay down a barrage so that Esposita could be rescued. For whatever reason.

Anna rode out ahead of the column, and even with the starlight limiting her vision, confidently led them around the bulge of the mountain and down a steep but wider trail, urging them on relentlessly. Out there on the flats below was a smudged cluster of lights.

'That where we're going?' he asked.

'*Sí*. El Carcel. It is a military prison full of political dissenters. There is supposed to be one wall that is painted red with the blood of men who have been executed.'

'We had a place called Andersonville that might've give it a run for its money.'

She stared across at him. 'The difference is, Link, that *our* man is prisoner out there. You *must* get him free! I — I will promise you — anything if you do this.'

He thought that if the light was better he might even see her face flushing. But he spoke curtly: 'You don't have to promise me a thing. And whether I succeed or not is in the lap of the gods.'

'No! It lies with *you*! You and the cannon. If you fail, I have no further use for either.'

She had said that so many times now that he was beginning to believe it. *She was capable of cold-blooded killing . . .*

She spurred away and he watched her. Just who the hell *was* this prisoner, really? He wondered whether he had been told the full story.

There was a narrow band of light, like a knife-blade seen edge-on, cracking the sky on the flat horizon as they set up the cannon on a piece of high ground not a quarter of a mile from the walls of the prison.

It was an oblong of adobe walls ten feet high, topped with barbed wire and broken glass. The gates were sharpened tree-trunks, cross-nailed with several wider, split trees to hold them together. The long hinges were hammered iron, black and shiny in the field glasses. This was desert: rust would not be a problem out here.

Lights were still burning, for it would be an hour yet before sunlight was strong enough to make them unnecessary. *They were running mighty close to the deadline.* There was movement, too. Guards at each corner of the wall were stirring, eager for the change of shift. Not that guard duty here would be a hard chore: there was little that threatened El Carcel. A violent sandstorm once in a while, maybe an occasional raid by renegade Indians, nothing more. It would not be easy to escape from, but guards had to be posted, and if they weren't any more alert than those down there, Davis thought, this raid might yet succeed.

Anna appeared beside him and he could see she was very edgy. 'Begin shooting, Davis!' she hissed. 'Why're you waiting? Daylight comes!'

He lowered the field glasses and spoke quietly to the four men who were to load and help him lay the cannon, adding for Anna's benefit: 'I need ranging shots, and that's going to stir 'em up like a hornet's nest.'

'It cannot be avoided?' He shook his head and she shrugged, took out her pearl-handled pistol. 'Start shooting.'

The men fumbled the cannonball after managing to ram home the bagged powder charge smoothly enough. One man howled as the heavy iron ball rolled across his bare toes in his sandals. Anna hissed at him, slashing with her quirt. The ball was loaded and Davis crouched behind the breech, to get line of sight. He figured that if the first ranging shots were going to stir up the Mexicans anyway, he might as well try to make them count for something.

So he aimed at the gate, had the men lift the carriage tail, swing it through a short arc to the right. He drove one more wooden wedge under the barrel, sighted again, aware that Anna was almost dancing with impatience.

As he teased the fuse-end carefully out of the touch-hole and took one more sight, Anna made a savage sucking sound. Unhurriedly, he applied his vesta. The fuse spluttered, showering sparks briefly, pungent smoke rasped his nostrils. Then the cannon leapt as the charge exploded, lancing a yard-long dagger of flame from the muzzle, and the ball whistled in an unseen arc to smash into the wall at one side of the gate.

'Load! *Pronto! Pronto!*' Davis yelled, sweating now.

The men fell over each other in their eagerness. The shot had chewed adobe from the wall, showering dust across the still-closed gates, but some of the wooden upright stakes had splintered, too. Anna cried encouragement as Davis had the men lay the gun's line of fire a little to the left.

There was excitement in the prison behind the walls, men shouting, a bugle sounding the alarm. The second shot thundered and the massive weight of the Dahlgren cannon shuddered, its wheels leaping. This time the gates smashed in, showering splinters and slivers of wood as tall as a man.

Anna and her men cheered, and before Davis could stop them they mounted and charged across the intervening ground, screaming abuse, shooting into the air, waving machetes, rowelling their mounts savagely, lusting to kill.

'Christ!' Davis swore. 'Now they're charging into my target area!'

He looked around just in time to stop his team from joining the main fight. He cuffed and swore and kicked them back to the cannon, practically thrust the powder charge and the rammer into their hands, almost threw a cannon ball at another man. Somehow the gun was reloaded and he lifted the muzzle with one more wedge, eased the carriage around this way and that, fired his shot, over the heads of the attackers. But it didn't quite clear the wall. It blew a ragged arc out of the top, from where barbed wire shrieked and writhed lethally, as it cut down three running guards.

While he shouted at the men to reload, Davis made himself slow down, trying to judge it just right this time. He could see the red-painted iron roof of the cellblock where Anna had told him Esposita was being held. He set his aim for the far end, where the entrance and guards' quarters were.

The cannon roared and leapt. When the smoke cleared he saw that the end of the cellblock had collapsed, blown into a pile of rubble. There was an entire corner missing, where iron roof-sheets twisted and clanged. *One more would do it!* he thought, but he wasn't going to get that finishing shot. The gun team had run for their mounts, impatient to join the others as they swarmed through the shattered gates into the prison yard, eager to start plundering and killing.

Davis ran towards his big black horse with the Mexican saddle, mounted stiffly, then spurred across the flats towards the slaughter that was taking place behind the damaged walls. Black smoke, shot through with flames, curled skywards. There were several explosions and he knew they were using dynamite. Beyond the shattered gates he could see Mexican guards being hacked and shot to death.

Then two riders cut out of a side gate and he hauled rein in surprise.

One was Chet Bradford and he was holding the other man in the saddle. This second man had a pale bandanna around his head, but he was limp and swaying and Davis knew he was wounded. Then the pair dropped out of sight over the lip of a huge crater. Davis had a decision to make: go to the prison where hell had come to visit? Or give chase to Bradford and his unknown sidekick?

He didn't know what Bradford was doing here but figured he had known about the prison's location and made for it after his abortive attempt to bushwhack Davis with Matheson. But who was the other man? *Who cared?*

Bradford had yet to pay for Benny Grant's death, that was what mattered.

He glanced back towards the jail, which was well ablaze now. Anna's men must have taken over: she would have found Esposita, barely alive or already dead. Either way, Davis had nothing to gain by joining her men in a slaughter for which he had no stomach.

But he still had his score to settle with Bradford.

And now was as good a time as any.

★   ★   ★

Inside the ruins of El Carcel, Anna Cortiz held firmly to the arm of a man in rags, his body and face marked with the scars of weeks of torture. His mangled feet dragged as Chico held him on the other side. They moved slowly along a stone passage, Anna's eyes filled with tears as she spoke quietly, encouragingly to the injured Esposita.

'A little more, *querido mio* — not far

now and you will have your revenge!'

The man lifted his ravaged face, damp, filthy hair spilling across his forehead marked with burns and bruises.

Coming towards them down the passage was a small group of rebels, flushed with the blood-pumping excitement of conquest. They dragged at a fat little ball of a man between them, ignoring his screams of fear and pleas for mercy.

General Almeida had soiled himself in his terror and his eyes bulged as he was halted a few feet in front of Esposita. The rebels held him while Anna took her pearl-handled pistol and worked it into the broken-fingered hand of Esposita.

'It is double-action, *querido*. Just pull the trigger . . . He is there in front of you. Can you see him?'

Esposita murmured something incoherent and she helped steady his hand. Chico supported his thin shoulders as he raised the pistol in both hands. It wavered. Almeida screamed, tried to run, was smashed in the face by a rebel and pushed back into the clear space. He started to fall to his knees, hands clasped in supplication — then the gun fired.

Again and again. Until the hammer fell on an empty chamber — and still Esposita kept pulling the trigger, murmuring something, the pain-filled eyes brightening briefly with what could only have been exhausted satisfaction.

They pulled him forward so he could look down on the blood-soaked Almeida's corpse.

Somehow he found enough remaining energy to spit on the remains of the man who had ordered the murder of his family.

12

Fathers and Sons

Bradford was waiting for Davis as he rode over the rim and down into the crater, once the outlet of a massive, ancient volcano. The saucerlike depression was scattered with hundreds of pieces of pumice ranging in size from a man's fist to that of a melon.

Black basalt boulders protruded at odd angles from the curving sides. And it was from within the shelter offered by a ring of these that Bradford fired his first shots.

His face scabbed and pocked from Davis's disintegrating bullet a few days earlier, Chet triggered rapidly. Davis lay low in the saddle as his big black swerved, gravel and pumice dust exploding around its front feet. He dropped out of the saddle, taking his

Henry with him, sliding it from the rawhide sling he had made to fit under his left leg when riding.

He rolled with more bullets raising dust around him. There wasn't much cover here but he squirmed in behind a low line of basalt, laid the Henry between two rocks and put two fast shots into Bradford's hiding-place. The lead struck sparks from the edge of one boulder, ricocheted away like a mad hornet. He saw Bradford jerk and duck back, startled at the placement of the shots. *Must've forgot I was a sharp-shooter before we formed the Trail Wolves*, Davis thought.

He levered a shell into the breech and lifted his upper body enough to see Bradford's shadow cast by the strengthening sunlight. His mind suddenly cleared, the buzzing disappeared, and he swiftly calculated which way Bradford was moving. He placed his next shot carefully between a narrow gap in the boulders. There was a yell, a clatter, and Bradford's shadow dropped out of sight. *Knocked him down or he slipped.*

Davis was already moving, jumping the low line of rocks, running and zigzagging closer to Bradford. The wounded man accompanying Chet, whoever he was, seemed to be right out of it, taking no part in the shooting. *One less gun to worry about.* Then Bradford rose between two rocks, pistol in hand this time, snapping two more shots at Davis.

The Texan sprawled and rolled in close against a small rock. The six-gun boomed again and a ball splattered against a flat plane of the rock, chips buzzing over Davis's head. His body was not completely hidden here and he knew he would have to move. Which meant making Bradford keep his head down while he did so. He twisted with a wrenching movement that made his muscles crack, eased the rifle down one side of the rock and put three raking shots into the ring of boulders. He heard the lead whining and buzzing around inside the circle and leapt up, running straight up the slight slope now. Afraid of breaking his stride and losing his rhythm, he didn't try to lever in a fresh shell on the run but concentrated on reaching the boulders before Bradford and his companion recovered from the menace of the deadly ricochets.

Breath burned in his throat. He stumbled as his boots slid on broken pumice, straightened and pounded on, drawing closer — closer. Now he was level with the boulders. He spun to his right, coming in across the slope.

Suddenly, he skidded and fell. When he righted himself as his rifle slid away down the side of the crater, he saw Bradford and the wounded man.

They were together beside one of the larger boulders. Bradford was standing but supported the other man, using him as a shield. His big six-shooter was raised, the muzzle pressed against the wounded man's temple. Davis crouched, waiting.

He could see the man's face: it was bruised and cut, had ragged lines of dried blood criss-crossing it. There was a crude bandage around his head, another dirty one almost entirely covered his left hand. He was being held upright mostly by Bradford's arms; his eyes were bewildered. Davis was surprised to see that he was a man in his fifties, face worn and contorted by some recent, ugly ordeal.

'Stay put, Davis! Or I finish him.'

'No skin off my nose.'

Bradford laughed harshly. 'Wouldn't be too damn sure about that! I been thinkin', Link. Mebbe I believe you when you say you never told that Yankee sergeant about our river crossin'. I recall you puttin' that spare map inside your cap, now, so it could've happened the way you said.'

'Too late, Chet. You let Keller kill Benny Grant.'

Bradford arched his eyebrows. 'Was that his name? Ah, to hell with it! I thought that headshot would've stopped you, but what the hell does it matter I believe you or I don't? You and me've been shapin' up for this for years!'

'Never saw it that way.'

'Hell, yeah! Had to happen from the moment we formed the Wolves. I had the rank, but you had the brains! You made me look a damn fool in front of the others a hundred times! You ever think about how that made me feel?'

'Can't say I did. Tried to leave you in charge, Chet, but just happened I knew the country better, was all.'

The wounded man groaned and Bradford curled a lip. 'Now *he's* gonna die on me, I s'pose! Damn! Nothin' works out for me. I got nothin' to go back to in Georgia, house an' kin're all gone. Din' get no money for them guns, rest of the Trail Wolves are dead — now I'm on the run. All your damn fault, Davis! An' I aim to put it to rights.' He lifted the six-gun and suddenly the wounded man slumped, whether by design or collapsing because of his wound it wasn't clear, but he pulled Chet off balance as he fell, just as Bradford's gun fired.

Davis dived left, feeling a burn in his side as he reached across his body for his own revolver, tearing it from the flapless holster. Bradford's gun thundered again and then Davis, sprawled on his belly now, fired two shots. They jerked Bradford up and half-twisted him. His scarred face was contorted in agony and fury. He made one last effort to throw down on Davis but a third bullet slammed him onto his back and he fell across the wounded man's legs. As he spilled off them, his eyes rolling up into his head, Davis heard him say clearly, between sobs of pain, 'Damn you — Dysart . . . '

Then Bradford died noisily and Davis struggled to his feet, looked up sharply as he saw riders lining the rim of the crater.

Anna waved. 'We have Esposita, Davis! We have won!'

He nodded, then sat down again,

heavily, feeling the warm blood sliding down over his ribs.

*　*　*

'Bradford called you 'Dysart',' Davis said, looking down at the wounded man, whose injuries had now been tended by Anna and Maria.

Wisely, they had moved away from the area of El Carcel soon after the raid. When Davis had come up out of the crater, pressing a hand against his bleeding side, he had seen what was left of the infamous prison. It was no more than a pile of rubble, flames and smoke drifting upwards from a dozen different places. The Dahlgren cannon had been blown apart by a charge of dynamite so the army troop which would inevitably be sent out here to investigate would not be able to use it.

Chico had led them all to another secret hideout, a two-day trek, and higher in the sierras this time, where the women and children were already waiting. The wounded were tended, including Davis, although his was only a scratch compared to some injuries others had sustained. He did not bother to ask if any of Almeida's men had survived the raid.

It had been the little *generale's* misfortune to be at El Carcel at the time of the raid. He had come to watch the execution of Esposita, the rebel who had defied the worst torture Almeida and his men could devise — but he had died instead at the hands of the prisoner, with a little help from Anna and Chico.

But Esposita was alive and recovering from his horrendous injuries. He was not a big man physically, but he was big on courage and determination.

Now, in a cave warmed by a fire kept at an even rate of burning by little Tonio Esposita, Davis hunkered down by the wounded man who had saved his life by distracting Bradford. The man had claimed it was not intentional: he had simply fainted at an opportune time.

'I was so blamed weak, my legs wouldn't hold me any more,' he said, his strong Yankee accent echoing around the cave.

That was when Davis said: 'Bradford called you 'Dysart'.' Adding: 'It's a name I've heard back in Texas . . . '

'My brother, Hammond, is Chief Commissioner of the Reconstruction in Texas,' the wounded man told him. 'I'm a politician and as Ham was having a lot of problems with you Texans, he sent for me to see if I could help find a solution. They call him 'Devil' because of his hard line but he's really a dedicated man, truly wants to make a success of the Reconstruction, see the South content to rejoin the Union, and make this one nation again . . . '

He stopped, smiling faintly. 'There I go, up on my political soapbox! Cutting corners, I travelled down here into Mexico as an unofficial ambassador. Washington knew nothing about it though I hinted that I had backing from there. A lot of Texans and Southerners in general are defecting and joining the Mexican revolution, because men like Governor Valdes are offering high prices for horses and fighting men. My brother saw this as a hindrance to the success of his Reconstruction vision, and also the fact that these men are taking US arms to the rebels. *That* does not look good on the political scene, here or overseas where several countries are showing an interest in what is happening in our land — and in Mexico, too, as witness the figurehead Emperor Maximilian, and soldiers of the French Foreign Legion fighting on his behalf.

'Ham is eager to have these things straightened out. There could be a real threat to the security of the United States from all this foreign activity along our border. He figured Valdes would want things clarified, too.'

'I'd reckon the same.'

Dysart smiled crookedly. 'Yes. Well, Valdes is all for putting down the rebels at any cost, but only if he can make a profit along the way.' He shrugged. 'Fact is, I caught him out in quite a bit of corruption and sort of hinted there could be official intervention by Washington, but I could see he wasn't going to fall into line. He was on too much of a good thing. But I left it too late to try to get out, dropped my veiled threats too soon. He sent me to a General Almeida in Coahuila Province on a pretext and the general, a man after Valdes's own heart — perhaps even on the Governor's instructions — took me hostage. He was asking for a hundred thousand US dollars for my safe return.'

'Did the fool know what he was doing? It could start another damn war between Mexico and the Union.'

'Oh, he knew, but greed took over. Anyway, I'd only just been taken to El Carcel when the young lady and her friends arrived.' He smiled up at Anna and even tried to bow from the waist up, lying as he was on his bedroll. 'I am forever thankful, ma'am. And to you,

Mr Davis. I'm afraid your friend Bradford was an opportunist, saw me as a way to easy money, too. He was no better than Almeida or Valdes, I'm afraid.'

'All snakes together. I can't go back to Texas now, Mr Dysart, but when you're well enough I could get you safely up to the border by some backtrails I know.'

Dysart looked at him thoughtfully and said, 'Why can you not return to Texas?'

Davis told him briefly about the trouble with the Rolling D. 'We had no choice, Benny Grant and me. We had to run but I couldn't go without making one last . . . protest.'

Dysart nodded and smiled when Tonio brought him a clay mug of coffee. Davis helped Anna get the man to a sitting position and the boy returned to tending the fire.

'So you stampeded your own cattle while they were being stolen. A fine piece of strategy, and irony, my friend. I believe I will accept your offer to escort me back to the border.'

Davis nodded, a little absently, sipping his coffee and watching the boy tend the fire. Anna straightened the blankets, started to rise, paused when she saw Davis studying Tonio. She was suddenly tense. 'What is wrong, Link?'

She had hardly even greeted the boy and Esposito did no more than squeeze Tonio's shoulder . . . something queer here!

Davis's eyes moved slowly towards Anna. 'The boy . . . reminds me of someone — that face like a young hawk, the shape of his nose and the brown eyes. I felt it before — it's come to me now that he reminds me of my father — or maybe even myself when I was about his age . . . ' His voice hardened a little. 'Just how old is he, Anna?'

Her face straightened and she was silent for a long time, her jaw clamped tight. She would not meet his eyes.

Dysart frowned, watching her, wondering at the long hesitation. Then she said in a barely audible voice: 'He will be eleven next month.'

Davis nodded gently. 'I wondered! You told me once he was only eight. But I thought he was kind of big for eight.' His eyes narrowed, his voice became steely. 'Did you lie to me when you said the baby had died ten years ago, Anna?'

As if she had previously reached a decision, she answered without hesitation now. She tossed her head a little, eyes flashing defiantly. 'All right! I lied!'

'Tonio is not Esposita's son, is he?'

'No. He is yours! He took the name Esposita when I married Vincente.'

Davis stiffened now. 'He's your husband . . . ?' *It explained a lot — her anxiety, wild mood swings — when they were attempting Esposita's rescue . . .*

'Yes, we were married a few years ago.' Still defiant, aggressive, she seemed almost eager for him to argue.

Davis swung his eyes back from watching the boy push more wood into the fire. 'Although you said Maria wasn't Tonio's mother, I had the impression that she had reared him, was still doing so.'

'Maria — and some of the other women.' Her voice was very quiet now.

'*You*'ve paid him little attention, Anna!'

She was breathing heavily now, her eyes cold. 'I did not want anything to do with him,' she said in a low voice so the boy would not hear — and Davis gave her full marks for that. 'He was — nice — but — he reminded me so much of *you!* And I did not want that!' She paused, breathless in her anger. 'You broke my heart and you broke your word to me! Oh, I know about your father's illness and the war! But *nothing* was a good enough excuse! You *should*'ve come back but you abandoned me! Left me with a child I didn't want. Maria was happy to rear him with her own brood when *El Tigre* was killed. I had the responsibility that went with his name and to continue his work to fight Valdes and men like Almeida. I did not want or need to have to worry about a child. Having him had already cost me so much!'

'For God's sake, woman!' exclaimed Dysart suddenly. 'I don't know all of what you're saying but I think I can put it together. Your own *son* was here, within sight and sound, within reach and you . . . ignored him? What kind of woman would — *could* do such a thing?'

She rounded on Dysart, glad of the diversion, someone to vent her mounting rage on. 'You know nothing! I was violated by this man Link Davis! I thought I loved him — but he threw me away like some local whore! Left me with the child — and to face my father's wrath alone! I did not want anything to do with any child of his!' Her eyes moved to Davis. 'I hated him! Still do!'

Dysart was looking at Davis now and

the Texan shook his head briefly. 'First I knew there was a child was a couple of weeks ago when I came down to Mexico — first time for ten years. Anna told me then the baby had died. I see why now: she had a use for me, after all.'

'You're an unforgiving woman, ma'am, but . . . this sounds all rather sad,' Dysart said heavily. 'If there's some way I can help either of you sort it out — '

'There is nothing to 'sort out'! Nothing has changed, except I have my husband back and he is alive and we will have some happiness together. Perhaps even children of our own!' Her eyes were brimming as she turned to Davis. 'I . . . used you, Link, yes. Why shouldn't I? You owed me *so much*! But I *am* grateful to you for helping me rescue Vincente. Perhaps I can even reward you. If you want Tonio, I have no objections . . . '

'Jesus, Anna! If I *want* him! My God, I'm on the run, can't settle anywhere in safety . . . ' He paused, seeing the boy studying him with those large brown eyes. Suddenly he felt a kind of hotness in his chest and the protests stuck in his craw. Then very different words tumbled unbidden out of his mouth, words he hadn't consciously thought of. He smiled, lightened his voice: 'Eh, Tonio. You like to come with me when I take Mr Dysart up to Texas?'

The boy, very serious, stared at him steadily, glancing in Anna's direction sombrely before eventually answering. '*Sí, señor*. I think I come. You have the look of Chico.'

Davis frowned at the scar-faced man who was leaning against the rock wall, smoking a cheroot. Chico shrugged.

'When there was time, I showed the boy some things that might help when he is growing up.'

'I hope they were good things?' Davis asked, a faint smile touching his lips.

Chico rocked one hand side to side. 'Mmmmm, some good, some not so good maybe — but all useful.' He

winked solemnly and Davis under-
stood. *'Useful' to a future rebel, he
meant.*

'*Muchas gracias*, Chico,' Davis said,
turning to Anna then. 'No one in his
right mind would leave the boy with
you, Anna. You're too damn bitter and
selfish — you use people, take yourself
too seriously. You'd be better going by
your given name instead of trying to
live up to *El Tigre's* — '

'I will run my own life, Davis!' She
clenched her fists down at her sides.
She was emotional, *too* emotional, and
quite unstable, Davis thought. It was
one hell of a life she was leading, too
much for her inexperience, getting by
on the loyalty of Chico and the men.
No doubt that was the cause of her
twisted outlook, but he felt there was
no excuse for her not wanting to be a
mother to Tonio. She knew this and he
felt that this was why she was so upset
now.

He grinned at the boy as he stood up.
'I'll be happy to take you with me,

Tonio. We'll have ourselves as good a time as I can make it. Likely won't be too much of a life, but it can't be worse than the one you'd have if you stayed here, and — we'll be together. That OK with you?'

'I come with you, *señor*,' the boy said emphatically, and Davis wondered if he would be able to live up to Tonio's expectations. He could but try.

'Link.' Dysart waited until Davis looked at him. 'I believe you will be able to go back to Texas. You saved my life no matter what you think to the contrary. I can repay you by recommending to my brother that all charges against you be dropped and your land be returned to you.'

'You're dreaming, Mr Dysart. Your brother won't listen. That stampede killed some Yankee soldiers . . .'

'No better than rustlers, Link, the kind of men the Reconstruction can do without. I'm not talking wild. I have a lot of influence with my brother and I believe you are the type of man he

251

wants to help resettle Texas. I will go on ahead, of course, once you get me to the Rio, and confirm it. But I would not have mentioned it if I didn't believe it will be so.'

Davis just stared for a while, then realized that Tonio was leaning against his leg. He tousled the boy's hair, smiling. 'We might just make a gen-u-ine Texican out of you yet, Tony.'

The boy grinned back widely.

Anna, behind him, looked sad, wiped at her eyes and suddenly smiled wanly at the boy. Her voice was barely audible as she said: '*Apenado*, Tonio. I'm . . . sorry.'

She turned abruptly towards the cave entrance. There was little show of reluctance but she did hesitate in the entrance for a moment. Then she strode away, not looking back, increasing her pace as she headed for the lean-to where Esposita lay on his bedroll. *Perhaps he could help her. A little genuine love and affection could work wonders . . .*

'Don't think too badly of her, Mr Dysart. She was mighty young, we both were, and her father expected a lot of her. Too damn much, I think.'

'So I gathered. It's one of the Old Spanish ways: if there is no son to carry on the father's work, then a daughter is chosen and she must find the strength from somewhere within herself. But I think the boy will benefit in the long run, being with you, Mr Davis. You're bound to get married some day.'

Davis started at that. It was something he hadn't thought about. But looking at the boy who stood close against him now, he figured it might not be such a bad idea.

He'd have to start looking.

When they got back to Texas.

We do hope that you have enjoyed reading this large print book.

Did you know that all of our titles are available for purchase?

We publish a wide range of high quality large print books including:
Romances, Mysteries, Classics
General Fiction
Non Fiction and Westerns

Special interest titles available in large print are:
The Little Oxford Dictionary
Music Book, Song Book
Hymn Book, Service Book

Also available from us courtesy of Oxford University Press:
Young Readers' Dictionary
(large print edition)
Young Readers' Thesaurus
(large print edition)

For further information or a free brochure, please contact us at:
Ulverscroft Large Print Books Ltd.,
The Green, Bradgate Road, Anstey,
Leicester, LE7 7FU, England.
Tel: (00 44) **0116 236 4325**
Fax: (00 44) **0116 234 0205**

Other titles in the
Linford Western Library:

THE JAYHAWKERS

Elliot Conway

Luther Kane, one-time captain with Colonel Mosby's raiders, is forced to leave Texas; bounty hunters are tracking down and arresting men who served with the colonel during the Civil War. He joins up with three Missouri brush boys, outlawed by the Union government, and themselves hunted for atrocities committed whilst riding with 'Bloody' Bill Anderson. Now, in a series of bloody shoot-outs, they must take the fight to the red legs to finally end the war against them . . .

VENGEANCE AT BITTERSWEET

Dale Graham

Always a loner, Largo reckoned it was the reason for his survival as a bounty hunter. But things change when he has to join forces with Colonel Sebastian Kyte in the hunt for a band of desperate killers. Kyte is not interested in financial rewards. So what is the old Confederate soldier's game? And how does a Kiowa medicine man's daughter figure in the final showdown at Bittersweet? Vengeance is sweet, but it comes with a heavy price tag.

DEVIL'S RANGE

Skeeter Dodds

Caleb Ross had agreed to join his old friend Tom Watson as a ranching partner in Ghost Creek, and arrives full of optimism. But he rides into big trouble. Tom has been gunned down by Jack Sweeney of the Rawl range, mentor in mayhem to Scott Rawl . . . Enraged, Caleb heads for the ranch seeking vengeance for Tom's murder. But, up against a crooked law force and formidable opposition, he'll have to be quick and clever if he's to survive . . .

THE COYOTE KIDS

David Bingley

When Billy Bartram met Della Rhodes, he was led to contact her brother, Sandy East, one of the Coyote Kids. Billy's determined vendetta against Long John Carrick — a veteran renegade and gang leader — made him an ally of the Coyote Kids. Carrick's boys were hounding them to grab some valued treasure, but only the Kids knew of its location. When Red Murdo, the other Kid became a casualty, Sandy and Billy had to fight for their very existence . . . as well as for the treasure.